# *Distant* BROTHERS

ROBERT E. KELLAR

**Wasteland Press**
Shelbyville, KY USA
www.wastelandpress.net

*Distant Brothers*
by Robert E. Kellar



First Printing – February 2010
ISBN: 978-1-60047-400-2



Printed in the U.S.A.

0 1

# CHAPTER ONE

## *New Somerton - Early August*

Homer Minley had grown up in New Somerton, a decaying little town a few miles up the Ohio River from Marietta. Homer wasn't real dumb. But then he wasn't real smart. His favorite past-time was roaming back through the wooded hills with Rover, his six-year old pooch. He figured Rover was about one-fourth hound, one-fourth beagle, one-fourth bird dog, and one-fourth mutt.

There had never been much time for sports in high school. Homer had worked in his dad's auto body repair shop for two or three hours every day after school as long as he could remember; and full time every summer.

Between junior and senior years in high school, he'd gotten in the habit of going to Marietta – that's where the action was – every Saturday evening, with Rodney and Dave, to look for things to do. It had become routine to start out at one of those coin-operated baseball batting cage facilities to try out their skills, then off to Cheater's Place, which was a great place for a beer – Cheater's didn't really check ID's very closely – and to pick up girls.

Over a period of several weeks, Ralph Croston, the owner of the batting practice facilities, and a former minor league player, had begun to notice that Homer almost never missed a pitch. And it didn't seem to matter at what speed the machine was set. He just hit every damned pitch that came at him. Not that Ralph watched customer skills very closely, but over time he had been taken by Homer's consistency.

Ralph's long-time friend, Frank Turlock, had stopped by while passing through Marietta one Saturday evening. Frank was a scout for the Boston Socialists major league team. He'd stop and have dinner with Ralph once or twice a year when in the area. But that Saturday evening, as Ralph went into his little wooden office shack to take a lengthy phone call, Frank, with nothing better to do, happened to observe Homer hitting high speed pitches from the machine; one after another, after another. "That kid's having a good night."

"That kid has had about 17 good nights in a row," replied Ralph.

Well the short of it was, that before Homer ever made it into his senior year in high school, he found himself in uniform for the final 14 games of the season with Boston's Class A farm club, the Texas Scrub Brushes. And although, they were unable to pull out of last place, the Scrub Brushes did win their final 14 games, and Homer hit a blistering .677.

Homer had never been outside that part of the Ohio Valley before. West Texas was all very confusing to him. It was all just scrub brush and flat boring country. He'd seen those bumper stickers, "Don't mess with Texas," and he wondered why anybody would want to bother. Besides, half his teammates didn't speak English.

A couple weeks later, Homer was happy to get back to Rover – he'd missed Rover – and to his senior year and his friends. Homer was a little slow to understand the process, but by late fall he began to realize that he really was expected to report to Boston's spring training camp in Florida in February. In spite of the problem that Homer was not a very good outfielder, he was outstanding at the plate. So the Socialists assigned him to their AA club, the Jersey Mob, to begin the season.

Homer hit exceptionally well his first couple weeks into the season. Although it was unusual for a minor league club to use a rookie as a designated hitter, he just couldn't field the ball "worth a hill-of-beans," according to Homer, so there was no place else to put him.

Other than spring training in Florida, Homer had never been east of the Ohio Valley so New Jersey was quite an experience for him. Crowds, traffic, fast pace – this wasn't like west Texas either.

On his first trip to Manhattan with three of his teammates one off-day, they decided to try out the subway from Penn Station up to Times Square. It was packed. Homer thought he was wedged right against the subway door until the train stopped at Times Square. Then he found himself suddenly wedged against the opposite wall with the crowds pouring past him up a set of gloomy looking stairs.

When the foursome finally emerged onto Broadway, they found things almost as hectic, and so as to find refuge to collect their thoughts, they edged their way down 43rd Street and into a modest looking restaurant. The help seemed awfully formal, and they didn't speak very good English. It surely wasn't much like Sally's Grill, the best lunch spot in New Somerton. But it was the check for $250 that Homer found most surprising. After a brief exchange of words, the four had paid the check on Homer's credit card. They promptly departed for New Jersey, not to visit New York again that season.

As the season progressed, the *Newark Star Ledger*, along with some of the other north Jersey papers, had begun to follow Homer's exploits at the plate with a mild interest. He was batting over .700 and had become a regular name in the sports pages.

But along about July rumors began to circulate that the ball club was having some "management" difficulties. When word finally came out that the Boston Socialists' management had been resistant, and finally refused, to make certain payments to a local organization for the right to operate in New Jersey, the Jersey Mob franchise ceased to exist.

In 71 games Homer had achieved a club record batting average of .781. "Phenomenal!!" according to the *Star Ledger*.

Homer did not understand what the fiasco was all about, but he was happy to go back home and take a long-needed trek through the woods with Rover. Nevertheless, good things don't last forever.

Only three days after arriving back in New Somerton, Homer got a call from Sean O'Daly, a big-wig in the Boston farm system. Next day Homer was on a flight to Minneapolis, home of Boston's AAA farm team. After Minneapolis had lost its major league franchise, Boston had jumped in quickly and secured minor league rights. And it was now home of the Minneapolis Socialists, namesake of its parent club.

Homer wondered if it wasn't confusing to have the same name but was comforted by the explanation. Boston had been concerned about fan support from the get-go; that was considering the bad feelings left when Boston's management had voted with the rest of the major league owners to pull the franchise out of the city. So when they established it as their AAA city, they had held a fan contest to name the new team.

As it turned out, the winning name had been submitted by a Minnesota congressman who felt that Minneapolis deserved equal "socialist" status with Boston, a point agreed to heartily by the judges. The congressman thus won a lifetime pass to all the Socialists, Minneapolis that was, home games.

Anyway, O'Daly had explained that the better players left hanging after the demise of the Jersey Mob franchise, had been sent to Boston's AA team – or at least an A team – to finish out the season, but that Homer, due to his incredible batting average, was to get a shot at AAA.

"Some things just don't work out, though," as Homer explained next day in a call to his dad from the Minneapolis airport. Apparently the whole Boston organization had a ton of good hitters, but a dismal dearth of pitching talent. So Homer had no sooner stepped off the plane arriving at Minneapolis, when he was traded to the Baltimore Flags of the International Universal League, in exchange for a couple of highly promising minor league pitchers.

He was promptly assigned to Baltimore's AAA team in Buffalo. The Buffalo Drifts had had a miserable season so far, with a team batting average of .167, and the Flags' management was desperate. So on a breezy, chilly evening in late July Homer suited up for his first AAA game at the near-empty ballpark in Buffalo.

44 games later, Homer finished the season with an astonishing .893 batting average and had been named "Player of the Year" in Buffalo.

The Drifts had climbed all the way up into fifth place, and attendance had escalated to over 300 fans per game. According to rumor, some senior management from Baltimore had visited Buffalo on a couple of occasions late season to observe this "probable flash-in-the-pan." In a couple of those games, Homer had actually gotten to play centerfield, but after dropping two fly balls, had been moved quickly back to designated hitter. Baltimore management was skeptical.

Nevertheless, right after Buffalo's season ended, Baltimore brought Homer up for the final game of the major league season at revered Ripken Field.

Things had happened so quickly that Homer's parents hadn't had time to make the trip to Baltimore. So there was Homer, all alone, in this huge city, kind of bewildered by it all.

Fortunately, the stadium was nearly empty for the game. Baltimore had finished solidly in last place, as they had for four straight years. And the Baltimore media had pretty much forgotten about baseball with the football season now coming on.

Only one or two of the Flag players had even said hello to Homer. He sat on the far end of the bench in the dugout, watching wide-eyed, as the despised New York Capitalists took a 3-0 lead into the eighth inning.

Butch Springfield, a grizzled and disgruntled has-been back-up catcher, seated next to Homer, hadn't said a word to him the entire game. Butch had accidentally spat a big splotch of tobacco juice on Homer's right shoe just as the home half of the inning started. And while Homer was quietly trying to clean his shoe, Bull Croggins, Baltimore's bulldog-faced sour-puss manager, had signaled for Homer to head for the on-deck circle to pinch-hit. It was a good thing Homer hustled. The previous batter grounded out on his first pitch.

As Homer stepped up to the plate, Roger Seneca, the Capitalists All-Star pitcher, glared. No way a rookie was going to spoil this no-hitter.

Down the pipe came the first pitch so fast that Homer had no time to duck. As he lay writhing in pain on the ground, the trainers first look gave fears that at least one forearm bone may be broken, hopefully nothing in the wrist.

At the hospital, x-rays revealed no broken bones. Homer had escaped his first at-bat in the major leagues with only a very badly bruised left forearm.

* * * *

That fall dragged on slowly back in New Somerton. His friends had all graduated from high school the previous spring and were now scattered hither and yon. Dave had enlisted in the Marines, and Rodney had gone off to college. One of Homer's ex-girlfriends was now married and another was pregnant. His dad had even hired a new guy to replace Homer in the repair shop so there was nothing much for him to do there.

Homer was the first one to arrive at Florida spring training camp that following February, and boy was he looking forward to it. At his age the physical conditioning came easy. He watched with near pity the overweight 30-some year olds struggle. It was good to be swinging the bat again. And he did it very, very well. Hank, the batting coach, was in near ecstasy by the end of the first week.

But Bull Croggins wasn't. Bull was short, stocky, gruff, and Type A, with a hair-trigger temper, and Homer soon began to fear that Bull might club him to death with a bat if he committed another error in the field. Only Hank's intervention saved Homer's life. Hank managed to convince Bull that since Homer was totally hopeless as a fielder, or any other place on defense, it wasn't worth a coronary. "Just assign him to permanent designated hitter status, and let me worry about him." Bull had enough other problems with a perennially last place ball club that he grumpily consented. And thank God Bull's attention was elsewhere after that, because Hank knew he faced monumental problems with Homer's ineptitude at base running and total inability to follow any coaching signals while at bat. Only a last place team could have endured a Homer. The fact was he almost never failed to get a hit when at the plate. That curiosity alone might draw some badly needed fans in Baltimore.

With a week to go in spring training the Flags had only won two games and heads were beginning to roll (off to the minors). Homer's two closest buddies by then were Jose Cuevas and Hark Adams. Jose was a solid third baseman, and he survived the cuts. But Hark's fortunes took a serious dip. Mid-week he got word that he was being sent down, not just to the AAA farm team in Buffalo, but to Baltimore's AA team, the Virginia Nicotines. Homer and Jose had a farewell beer with Hark and assured him that he would be back up with them by mid-season.

Although Homer's .890 batting average was not a good indicator – he hadn't had that many at bats – Hank managed to protect him from the cuts. So it was pack up and head for Baltimore, with only a day to get a locker assignment at Ripken Field, get briefly into a temporary apartment, and get packed for the trip to Chicago for the opening day game. The Flags would be in Chicago for their first two games, then on to Detroit for three more, before returning to Baltimore for an opening home game against the Atlanta Confederates.

Homer sat next to Jose on the flight out. And although Jose was starting his third season with the Flags, and must have seen a variety of flying and weather conditions, Homer could tell his Latin buddy was a bit nervous as the plane had to circle O'Hare Airport for nearly an hour waiting out a spring blizzard which had temporarily closed all but one of the runways.

Homer's parents had planned to drive to Chicago for his first full major league game, at least as full as a designated hitter could play, but the dire weather forecast caused a change in plans. They'd travel to Baltimore for the home opener the following week instead. Homer was glad, because it really was windy and bitter as the team arrived at their hotel that evening. In fact, the snowfall had picked up and driving conditions were poor.

At breakfast next morning, Jose predicted that "This game won't happen. Not today; not like this." An hour later the announcement came. The game would be postponed due to snow and would be part of a double-header in June. The rest of the day was spent reading the sports pages, drinking coffee – except Jose who described it as "coffee-flavored water" – and talking baseball.

By midmorning the older veterans had drifted off to do whatever veterans do in other cities. The rookies and younger players had split off into pairs and small groups to find things to do. Some surmised what Bull Croggins would do to the weather service people if he could chase them down with a bat, and others what he would do to any of them if he caught them drinking too much beer that afternoon.

By noon next day the sun was bright and the snow pretty much melted. The game was to be played as scheduled: Game time 7:30 p.m. Homer agreed with Jose that an afternoon game would have been smarter. "C'est la vie," whatever that meant, according to Brett Castle, a utility infielder who had played four years at Clemson before joining the Flags organization. Homer thought Brett was a nice guy, but never understood half of what he was talking about.

The Chicago Wind Chills did not have a sell-out crowd for their home opener that night. In fact, the stadium only looked about one-third full by end of the opening ceremonies. It was cold! An Irish band had played what resembled the National Anthem, and the mayor had delivered a political speech, while the players' teeth chattered in the dugouts. As it turned out, the whole scene finally did culminate in a baseball game, and Homer finally got his chance. Game time temperature 38 degrees.

Top of the second, Homer stepped up to the plate. Bill Byesvale, the Wind Chills starting pitcher, had begun to settle down, and the pitches were steaming. Homer took ball-1. Byesvale was feeling out this highly-touted rookie. Ball-2. Byesvale screwed up. He hadn't meant that one. The next one, a fast ball, came zinging down the center of the strike zone. And with a resounding crack of the bat went towering over the left field wall.

Homer circled the bases to the silence of the crowd and was met by a welcomed cheery enthusiasm as he crossed the plate into a small crowd of his teammates.

Bull Croggins hadn't budged from the dugout, but even he looked less fierce than normal.

The Flags held the 1-0 lead as Homer stepped up in the top of fifth with two out. Homer took the first strike – ump was losing his vision – then two straight balls. Byesvale was trying to bait him. Homer shouldn't have swung at the next pitch. Byesvale was working on him now. Foul ball. Next, a slider coming just over the knees and Homer slapped a single into right field.

Two pitches later and the inning was over, as Arley Lancaster, the Flags second baseman, flied out to center.

A burst of light snow flurries swirled around the field as the teams switched. Homer was happy to get back to the dugout where he could bundle up in a jacket. He was thankful not to be playing on defense.

By the top of the eighth the official temperature on the field was 36 degrees. Wind chill was well below that. Most of the fans had departed with the Flags still holding on to a 1-0 lead. Homer was the lead-off batter.

Byesvale's fast pitch, an 89 mph fast ball, came right over the center of the plate and went soaring right out against the fence in right center. Even at Homer's extraordinarily slow speed, he made it to second. Byesvale was sent to the showers. He had walked two batters in the seventh, and the cold temperature was getting to him.

After an interminable delay, waiting for the reliever to make his way in to the mound and take his warm-up pitches, while Homer was shivering his butt off out on second, the game finally resumed. After a strike-out, the Flags now had one out with Homer on second.

Billy Clark, the Flags fiery shortstop, was up. Billy got the count to 3 and 2, then whacked four straight foul balls. Homer recollected that he hadn't been that cold since he was out on a camping trip with a group of his buddies back about age ten and had forgotten his sleeping bag.

All Homer knew about the next pitch was that he had heard the bat connect with the ball. So he left second base and headed for third. The Wind Chills shortstop made an easy catch of Billy's pop-up, fired the ball to the second baseman; Homer, thinking there were two outs, headed for third and was easily doubled off the base. For a brief moment as the Wind Chills players quickly headed for their dugout, Homer was left in lonely bewilderment on the field. The stunned Flags team had not yet charged out for the bottom of the eighth. There was some kind of violent turmoil going on in the dugout. Although Homer couldn't see all of it, apparently Bull had thrown a major tantrum, had smashed the water cooler, broken two bats, accidentally knocked the batboy unconscious, and was headed out with a bat to destroy Homer when some of the coaches and players, at heavy personal risk, were able to restrain him.

Hank was able to quickly usher Homer into the club house behind Bull's back while some of the team were still struggling to settle him down. Fortunately, the Flags went on to win the game 1-0, and the team doctor managed to get enough sedatives into Bull that no further harm was done.

Next morning, back in Baltimore, the *Sun*'s sports page touted the Flags' pitching staff with heroic efforts, having won their first opening game in six years. As a lightly sarcastic side note, there was a small photo of Homer being doubled off base with the subscript, "Rookie!!"

On the flight to Detroit next morning, Jose pointed out that so far this had been the Flags most successful road trip in his memory, having escaped Chicago with one victory and one snow-out. Homer was grateful that a warm front was pushing through as they arrived at their hotel in Motown for a three-game series with the Detroit Lemons.

## CHAPTER TWO

# *Wilmington – Mid April*

"Dammit, Bibbie! Dammit, dammit! Why, why, why, you…? God dammit, Bibbie!"

About a year and a half old -- chubby little bastard. Loved to play in the park. Loved to make a mess of ice cream. And loved to fall asleep in my lap. He bawled so long one day when I stopped pushing him in the swing set I was about to leave him there. After all, his sister would eventually show up. But he had suddenly stopped, cooed, and jiggled his arms and legs in a flurry of toddler joy.

It had bothered hell out of me that he could con me like that. Because I didn't like kids. I didn't like kids one damned bit. I was 28 when I had moved to Wilmington after getting out of the hospital. Permanent disability -- but I could move around okay. It was cleaner and quieter than Philly.

My live-in before the accident had moved there while I was in the hospital, and I was just trying to track her down. But she had moved on again, and I wasn't up to the chase.

*#3 Minley*

*#2 Bogdan*

*#1 Kallister*

I had moved into a small third floor apartment in a big old brick building on a narrow tree-lined street near downtown. Spent a couple of hours every afternoon sitting on the front steps, watching people try to ease their cars in and out of the tight parking spaces without scraping their bumpers.

One Saturday afternoon that first week an eight-year old girl had dragged her baby brother out to the front steps—to get away from a screaming match between their mother and her boyfriend up on the second floor. She spent a couple of minutes at some eight-year old girl hop-scotch type motions on the nearby sidewalk while the toddler worked his way up and down the steps and the wrought iron rail on the other side from where I was sitting.

"Whata you sitting out here for, mister?"

I hoped my glare would let her know it was none of her damned business, but she kept looking right at me.

"Just resting."

"Where do you live?"

"Third floor," I answered, looking away from her, hoping she'd bug-off.

By that time the toddler had worked his way across the steps and had grabbed my sleeve to avoid tumbling down, all the while slobbering all over himself, my sleeve, and everything else in sight. Son-of-bitch, I had moved here for peace and quiet, not for hassles with a bunch of goddamn brats!

The screaming match coming out of the second floor seemed to have quieted down. Maybe the brats would go back up. I stood up hoping for that anyway.

"You almost made Bibbie fall when you stood up that fast."

"Well he didn't fall," I answered.

"But he almost did — and he could have hurt himself."

"Then why don't you take him back inside where he won't fall?"

"We can be out here as much as you can," she whined.

I was steaming. Taking that sort of lip from a little bitch like that. I stepped down to the sidewalk, stretched, and would have taken a walk just to get the hell out of there, but really didn't want to — why the hell should I have to do something I didn't want to just to get away from those two?

"Why are you limping, mister?"

"I hurt my leg." Damn!

"How did you do that?"

"It was an accident."

"That's how Bibbie hurt his back -- in an accident -- at least that's what Dack said," she mumbled.

By that time, Bibbie -- what kind of an asshole name was that? -- had worked his way down the three steps to the sidewalk and had toddled a ways back the narrow old concrete driveway that separated our building from the one next door. He had tripped and fallen forward, landing on his hands and knees, bawling so the whole neighborhood could hear.

Maybe it was out of instinct to help somebody who had been injured, but more likely so nobody could accuse me of not helping — or even worse, of maybe *causing* the kid to get hurt. Anyway, I followed his sister back to make sure he was okay.

His grubby little t-shirt had pulled up his back far enough that I could see a large welt, mostly healed, running across his lower back. She helped him up, brushed off his hands and knees, and half-carried, half-dragged him back to the front steps. The little bastard finally stopped whimpering and settled down to tapping away at the wrought iron with a small stick he had found under the rail.

An ice cream truck had rounded the corner, playing its endless little ditty, and had stopped for a small group of kids two buildings down from us. Funny that a 28-year old could still love ice cream, but it was one of my weaknesses. I got myself in line behind a mother and her brat who took forever to make up his mind.

"Yes, sir," the attendant offered.

"I'll have a cone with the chocolate and nut topping."

"$1.50," as he handed me the cone.

I paid him and headed back up the sidewalk, cursing as I lost a couple large pieces of the topping to the ground.

"What did you get?," the little bitch asked before I had barely sat down.

"A cone."

"What kind of a cone is it?"

"Ice cream."

She ignored my sarcasm.

They both sat silently staring at me as I battled to eat the top part of the cone without losing any more of the chocolate and nuts. Meantime, the truck had passed us, moving a short distance up the street, stopping for another small group of kids. I wished to hell it had kept on going.

Eventually Bibbie edged over closer to me and held out his hand for me to give him some. I turned slightly the other direction and concentrated on the cone.

More and more kids seemed to keep on coming to line up at the truck. It looked like it would be there forever.

Bibbie was haunting me now. I hadn't heard any racket from the upstairs window for some time, and I wished their mother would call them or come get them. Damn it.

"Bibbie wants a bite of your ice cream, mister."

There was no place else nearby to go sit. And even if there was, they would probably follow me.

"Leave the man alone, Bibbie," she whined as she tugged him back toward her side of the steps.

"Bibbie!" This time she screamed at him.

"Mister, could we get some ice cream?" she ventured after a few moments of quiet.

Damned if I was giving her the money. Where the hell was her mother? They'd be at me every day from now on if I gave her the money.

"Go get some money from your mother."

"I ain't goin' up there and get yelled at!"

Bibbie was working his way toward me again.

"Can't you get us just one ice cream, mister, and I'll share it with Bibbie?"

What a pain in the ass.

"I don't have any more money," I barked. "And even if I did, you go get your own."

"I saw the ice cream man give you some change!"

That did it. I stood up.

"Look, would you two get the hell out of here and stop pestering me!"

She had a little bit of moisture in her eyes as she slowly pivoted her body around to the outside of the opposite rail to pout.

"Bibbie, get over here," she scolded lightly.

In all this time Bibbie hadn't uttered any word that meant anything. I would have thought by the time a kid was his size he could say something you could understand what he was getting at. But not Bibbie.

"Ba, ba, ba…ba, ba, ba."

"Da, da, da! Da, da, da. Da, da, da, da."

"Then maybe it was better the little bastard couldn't say words. Then I'd have had both of them at me." His sister was enough of a pain in the butt as it was.

"You're mean, mister."

"Probably," I said.

"You could get us just one ice cream."

"God damn! Heaven has got to be a place without brats," I muttered to myself.

"If you two aren't going inside, then I am." I got up to leave.

"Well, we're glad, aren't we, Bibbie."

I paused, fumed, and headed in the door. "Son of a bitch…" I mumbled.

"Thank God Charlotte hadn't had any kids. At least not while I was married to her."

* * * *

The next day when I went out to sit on the front steps, Arsha (I heard her friend call her) and a friend of hers were playing jump rope in the street, occasionally pausing to move toward the sidewalk to let a passing car get by. They had left Bibbie playing with a broken piece of plastic tail-light at the bottom of the steps.

"That's that mean-ass old so and so who wouldn't give us any ice cream yesterday."

"Why wouldn't he?"

Arsha and her friend were whispering, but I could pretty well pick up the gist of it. Luckily, Bibbie kept on playing, not bothering with either me or the girls. Maybe I'll get some peace for a few minutes.

Four boys, ranging in age maybe from about eight to ten were making a nuisance of themselves across the street, pestering some poor dog with a stick. The dog was small, and after a while one of them picked the dog up and started to carry it up the fire escape of the old brick apartment house almost directly across from me. The dog just wagged its tail and licked the kid on his arms.

The kid coaxed his buddies to follow him as he climbed up on past the second floor window. I figured the little bastards probably intended to leave the dog up top to find its own way down.

I couldn't tell exactly what they were saying to each other, but a couple of them did taunt the kid carrying the dog as a "chicken." They probably weren't saying much of anything else other than a bunch of "likes" and "you knows" combined with an endless range of four-letter words. They all followed him up to the top of the fire escape at the fourth floor. A toothless old woman glowered at them out a third floor window, but didn't say anything.

Meantime Arsha and her friend kept their jump rope going at a furious pace. And Bibbie was still totally busy with his broken plastic.

"What the hell are they up to now?" I wondered.

Suddenly the dog came hurtling down! They had thrown it off the top of the fire escape. I watched, momentarily helpless. It hit the sidewalk with a thud and a sickening yelp! God damn! The poor little pooch had never had a chance from the time that rotten bastard kid first picked it up!

"What in the hell!"

A woman and a man had been walking down the sidewalk that side of the street and were just about 20 feet or so from where the dog had landed. They had not been near enough to see how the whole scene had developed and were instantly bewildered by the thud. The man looked up to see where the dog had fallen from. The boys were scrambling down the fire escape, half shouting in glee.

The woman went quickly to the dog, but there was nothing to be done. It had whimpered once, followed by a couple of twitches, and then went silent.

"How did that happen?" She started to cry.

The man went to her, half watching the boys clammer down.

"Oh the poor little thing," she sobbed.

"You call me a chicken now?" the scum-brat yelled at his buddies as they darted up the street and escaped.

By this time Arsha and her friend had run over to the woman to see what had happened and had gone into their exaggerated emotional fits that girls that age do. I went limping over, hoping to figure out some way to nail those little bastards, rather than expecting to be of any help.

"What a terrible, terrible thing!" The woman was still sobbing lightly. Her man just kept looking at the dog, at her, and at the direction the boys had run.

"Do you know those boys? Do they live around here?" The man was quizzing Arsha. Then he looked at me, all wide-eyed and tense.

I didn't know them, and Arsha may have been too scared to say.

"Should we call the police?" The woman looked first at her man and then at me.

"I'd like to drop the little bastard who did it off the top of that fire escape," I muttered.

"Got a cell phone?" the man pressed.

"Probably in that grocery store down at the corner," I pointed.

"C'mon, Martha. Let's go report this to the police."

I wandered back across the street to take my seat on the steps. Arsha and her friend had followed slowly after me, jabbering about who those boys might be and what school they were probably from.

Bibbie had been alone all this time at whatever the hell he'd been into. Luckily it didn't seem that he'd tried to come out into the street by himself, although no cars had been by for a while. He was fooling around with something in that corner of the sidewalk where the front steps joined the house. Arsha went over to check on him.

"Momma! Momma!" the little bitch started screaming as though a catastrophe had hit.

One of the second floor windows above us ripped open followed by a stream of vulgarities from their mother. Arsha yelled up to her that Bibbie had "done it again in his pants!" After a few more vulgarities, things went quiet for a few seconds until we heard her rushing down the stairs, slippers clattering, swearing and grunting. I moved to the iron rail as the screen door flew open.

I had barely gotten out of the way as she, panting and cursing, went straight for Bibbie. Arsha had quickly backed off, with both hands over her mouth in an expression of stark terror I couldn't tell was real or just young girl brat exaggeration. After all, it was her damned tattling which had triggered things. Somehow I wished her mother had gone for her instead of Bibbie.

The next few moments I'll never forget. As his mother grabbed his arm dragging him up the steps, his need to scream, or at least whimper, seemed to freeze. But his eyes – God, his eyes. Although it couldn't have been more than a couple of seconds, the agonizing terror he drilled right into *my* eyes, as though I might save him, was haunting.

I had only seen Bibbie's mother a few times since I'd moved into that building. We had never actually met. She'd never looked at me. Always in a rush.

She looked like one of those women who tried too hard to look like some sex cat, but in her non-stop rushing around always left herself a mess. I had started to say, "Good morning" to her once when she was coming up the steps while I was sitting out front. But she didn't even look sideways. She never looked sideways, always just a glazed glare straight ahead. She just charged right into the house, clattered up the stairs, and slammed the apartment door behind her.

And this time, as she dragged Bibbie up the stairs, she'd been pretty much the same. Just snarling more.

Bibbie was whimpering as I heard his little body bumping each of the stairs. But he couldn't seem to quite get a scream out in between gasps. After the apartment door had slammed, I thought I had heard one brief scream. But then there was sort of a muffled sound of another door inside their apartment slamming and everything went quiet.

Arsha had quickly disappeared about the time her mother had first grabbed Bibbie. Once the racket was over, she came quietly easing back around the corner of the building, looking half scared and half curious. I sort of felt that way myself. We probably both wondered what had happened up there to Bibbie. And why it was so quiet now.

It was times like this I'd think I should find some place other than those front steps to sit during the day time. But it was so relaxing just to sit there in the sunshine looking up and down that quiet street at the old brick apartment buildings and at the trees up and down both sides of the street. And then it all goes to hell with Bibbie and Arsha and their freak-ass mother, and all their commotions.

Of course, things were even worse on that street I lived in Philly. I don't remember any brats Bibbie's age. But the older ones were just damned mean. Rotten! Just didn't want to be around them. And they'd throw all kinds of trash all over the place.

We weren't like that when I was growing up in New Somerton. Or our parents would have beaten hell out of us. We just played ball. And fooled around the gas station where Mike worked. And things like that. But we didn't cause all kinds of problems.

"Mister?" Arsha never asked me my name. Just always called me "Mister." "What do you think she did to Bibbie?"

I didn't answer. Since it was quiet up there, I had hoped she'd just locked him in the bedroom and let him go to sleep.

"I bet she punished him." Arsha paused a while. "Pretty bad."

I just looked off in the distance and thought about those miserable brats who had dropped the little dog and what I'd like to do to them.

"My mother gets so mad at Bibbie sometimes. One time she threw him down on the bathroom floor so hard he just laid there for a while. Then he finally started crying. Then she just screamed at him. He makes her so mad when he doesn't do what he is supposed to do." She paused for a little bit.

"One time he burned himself on the heater, and I thought she was going to throw him out the window. I think she and Dack was drunk. They get drunk all the time. Or they were sniffing stuff. They do that a lot too. Sometimes it makes them crazy. I just sneak out of there. I don't think they know anyway. I don't like Dack. He's mean. One time he hit Bibbie so hard on his back he had a big welt for a long time. Bibbie screamed so loud she locked him in the bedroom until he stopped."

I wished she'd shut up. Even though I don't like brats, I didn't want to hear about this any more. Who wants to hear about creatures like Arsha's mother beating hell out of toddlers?

I wondered if they ever beat Arsha? At least she hadn't said anything about it. And I couldn't see any scars. But then a girl that age might be too embarrassed or too scared to say anything. Besides, by her age she may have learned how to protect herself by making sure Bibbie took all the hits. Anyway, her mother seemed like a complete bitch. And this guy Dack probably wasn't much different.

"Do you know how to play hopscotch, Mister?"

"No." Getting right to the point with her may shut her up.

Arsha just gazed down at her shoes, pivoting back and forth around the wrought iron rail post at the bottom of the steps on the other side. After a while she stopped and slowly wove her way onto the sidewalk, all the while just looking down -- and thinking. Her buddy she had been playing with earlier had long since left.

"I could teach you."

My mind was still off in a daze, wondering what had become of Bibbie up there. Poor little bastard. So I didn't answer her for quite a while. I was about to snap back at her but caught myself.

"Where's your friend you were playing with here earlier?"

"I don't know," she said.

After a long bit of trying to play slow motion hopscotch by herself, she paused for a little, all the while still just looking down at her shoes.

"It's easy to learn."

24 hours earlier I'd have snarled at her pretty hard. But I was just out of the mood. Maybe she was wearing me down.

"Not now," I told her.

She just kept shuffling around the sidewalk looking down.

"Why don't you go find your friend?" I still tried to sound a little gruff. "She can play hopscotch with you."

Arsha started to answer but was cut off by a loud slam of a door inside. A male voice shouted a couple obscenities which I couldn't quite understand. Down the stairs he charged, nearly ripping the screen door off its hinges. Thank God neither Arsha nor me was in his way. He went down the front steps in two leaps cursing and muttering to himself. Damn!

"What the hell is his problem?"

"That's Dack." Her lip was quivering.

"Well, what's his problem?" I was gruffer than I shoulda been, I guess. She turned her back to me and didn't answer. I could tell she was hiding tears.

What little I'd seen of Dack's face it was fierce as hell. That glassy-eyed, deadly, desperate look. As though he was on a combination of something. Who knows what kind of drugs he and the *bitch* were into. "What kind of a drug hole apartment house have I gotten into?"

After a bit, I slowly got up and started to go inside, up to my apartment. To escape I guess. I hated to sit inside in a crummy little apartment when the weather was nice.

"Where you goin', Mister?"

Wasn't it pretty clear where I was goin'? And what the hell business was it of hers? And why the hell did she care anyway?

"I'm goin' up to my apartment for Chrissake!" Took me a while to get up the stairs, my bum leg and all. It was quiet as hell as I passed by Arsha's mother's apartment door. Creepy.

The old wallpaper in the stairwells smelled musty. Probably hadn't been changed in 50 years. I swore at my key as it stuck in the rickety old lock. I always had to jiggle like forever to get the damn door open. I went over to raise the blind on the front windows so I could see out onto the street, along with the front stoop steps. The little bitch was still down there pouting.

From behind the trees lining the opposite sidewalk, Dack came cutting diagonally across the street toward the front steps. Long dark greasy hair, grubby battered t-shirt with rap jargon all over it. No expression, just looking straight ahead. He had a small white plastic bag in one hand.

Arsha had her back to him and didn't see him coming. He moved quickly past her, not as much as even glancing at her, two bounding steps up to the stoop, and slamming the door behind.

I turned around and just stood there for a while talking to myself. "I gotta find some place else to spend my days. Get away from those brats and their miserable mother and miserable Dack and the whole crummy scene."

The doctor had said I should walk some everyday. Keep my leg loosened up some. I hadn't looked around the neighborhood since I'd moved in. "Maybe there is a park bench or some place nearby where I can sit and relax. I gotta do something."

I looked out the window again. Bibbie was back down there with Arsha. "Well at least the little bastard's okay."

## CHAPTER THREE

# *Detroit – Mid April*

This was to be an afternoon home opener for the Lemons (their first two games they had split 1-1 on the road), and boy, had the city gone all out for the ceremony. The weather cooperated and so did the fans. Homer had never seen such a huge crowd. There were upwards of 30,000 people.

During pre-game warm up, Homer tried to stay as far away from Bull Croggins as possible. Actually, he'd been doing that ever since the eighth inning the night before. During warm up, Hank had personally thrown a few practice pitches for Homer to hit. Hank may have just wanted to be nearby to give Homer comfort. But Bull was way too busy with all the other things a manager has to worry about to bother about Homer. After all, it had just been a "rookie mistake."

Following warm up, the city had planned its usual opening ceremonies extravaganza. This year's sponsor was General Vehicles Corporation, who spared no cost. There were bands and fireworks and a beauty pageant and a grand finale parade to lead up to the speeches to open the new season. Leading the parade was a whole stream of General Vehicles' exciting new models for the following season: the Strumpet, a dashing red sports car with mach 1 acceleration, woven buckeye skin upholstery, and super boom-box grade sound system which could be heard across into Canada; the Ecstasy, an astounding luxury four-door sedan with satellite instruments to open your garage doors 200 miles away, start your dinner, pour your cocktail, and interrupt the x-rated movie your kids were watching, with a video-phone message from mom or dad; a huge six-door SUV, rated at 5.5 miles per gallon (highway) with built-in pool table, table tennis, and mini-golf; all led by General Vehicles' sole surviving 1921

Model P.

The crowd roared as each vehicle was greeted into the stadium by a bevy of beauty queens. Homer was enthralled. To think, he was a part of all this. He figured he might just go out and get himself one of them Strumpets as soon as he got back to Baltimore.

The Model P slowed to a crawl as it approached the speaker's stand, allowing the other vehicles to group up into a tightly-knit entourage for the culminating ceremony. But just as the P passed the center part of the platform, the Ecstasy's engine abruptly failed with such a jerk that the driver of the Strumpet, following close behind, had to hit the brakes which totally failed (wretched computerized system, thought some of the old timers in the stands), thus plowing into the rear of the Ecstasy. Unfortunately, the SUV driver, following even more closely behind, didn't have time to brake, and upon swerving abruptly to the left to avoid a collision, rolled over onto its top.

This all had happened so fast, while the roar of the crowd had nearly drowned out the crunching sounds, that the driver of the Model P had proceeded on around to the home team dugout area, tooting his horn in celebration, oblivious to the disaster behind.

Although the emergency van came careening out with sirens at full blast -- nearly ran down two panicked officials -- the only injury recorded was a twisted knee of one of the overweight paramedics who had jumped too quickly from the van. Otherwise, none of the General Vehicles drivers were seriously injured.

To Homer's dismay, the Strumpet had been totaled. There was about $5,000 in damage to the Ecstasy, and a little less than that to the super SUV. Some of the more unruly fans had bombarded the entire scene of wreckage with hundreds of lemons. Homer concluded that this had to be the most exciting event he'd ever attended.

By the time they had gotten wrecking trucks in to clear the mess, and the grounds' crew had had time to do their thing, the game delay had exceeded over an hour. Homer had been pleased with the entertainment -- not Bull Croggins. He'd been pacing the dugout the entire time wondering what the "h" baseball was coming to.

As Homer came to bat with two on and one out in the top of the second, Detroit held a 1 to 0 lead. Homer stood watching the first two pitches called strikes. He was still thinking about that Strumpet. Then he took two balls. On the next pitch, Homer's precision swing of the bat sent the ball up against the left center field wall and both runners scored. The next Flags' batter grounded out so Baltimore led 2 to1 after two.

It stayed that way until the top of the fourth when Homer whacked a single into right field scoring a runner from third. And with the Flags leading 3 to1, he singled again in the sixth inning, sending two more runners across the plate. Baltimore 5, Detroit 1. But in the bottom of the seventh, the Lemons scored four runs, sending the Flags' starting pitcher to the showers.

Top of the eighth, score tied. Homer stepped up to the plate with his buddy Jose on second base. First pitch, way outside, ball 1. Next pitch, high and outside, but Homer fouled it off behind first base. Bull grumbled some profanities to Hank next to him in the dugout. Homer had swung at a terrible pitch.

Next pitch, low and inside, ball 2. The signal was for Homer to hit toward right field. It was only due to Jose's remarkable speed that he managed to score from second as Homer hit a soft liner to short left field. The left fielder had fired the ball just a pinch too high for the catcher to make the tag at home. Baltimore 6, Detroit 5.

And that's how it ended, with Baltimore starting its season with 2 and 0, their longest winning streak in three and one-half years.

That evening all of Baltimore's TV sports reporters surmised that Bull Croggins may just be finally turning things around – too early to tell. And the Sun ran a front page (sports) photo of Jose sliding home for the winning run.

Game two in Detroit. Second inning, nobody out. Andre Matamoras, catcher, the Flags only All-Star from the last two years, was on second. Homer stepped up to the plate. First two pitches, way outside; count 2 and 0. Maybe they're on to him. But Charley Foulks's ego couldn't stand it. Star lefthander for 14 years, he wasn't letting this damned rookie at the plate control him. And Homer missed the third base coach's signal that he was to take the pitch.

Fastball, right down the center. Homer's bat split into pieces as he sent a ground ball steaming down between second and short, at least until it hit Andre's left ankle on his first stride toward third.

After the team physician had administered painkiller and other medical repairs, Andre was removed on a stretcher – out for the season.

For the first few moments after the incident, along with all the others gathered ‘round him, Bull’s entire focus of attention was on those early critical steps needed to deal with the injury.

Thank God, for Homer’s sake, Hank’s mind was one step ahead. While the stretcher was being hustled out, Hank took Homer by the arm and quickly got him into the clubhouse, dressed (without a shower), and out the exit to a nearby taxi. He arranged for Homer to be moved ASAP to a different hotel where Bull wouldn’t be able to locate him. Thus, Homer’s life was saved.

Back at the ballpark, Bull’s blood pressure hadn’t begun to soar until he watched the stretcher disappear into the dugout exit. Fortunately, Hank had made sure the umps had been notified as to the pinch runner for Homer Minley at first base. After his frantic efforts to hunt down Homer for execution had failed, Bull’s rage was released by the destruction of several lockers, various equipment paraphernalia, and all of the toilet seats in the visiting team clubhouse at Detroit stadium.

The Flags lost that second game by a score of 5 to 4, and their two-game winning streak was ended. Homer’s whereabouts was top secret, and Bull was given heavy sedatives for a good night’s sleep.

In the sports reports that evening, the Baltimore media focused almost entirely on the unfortunate loss of Andre Matamoras with only minor afterthought commentary on Homer’s mishap. Only a writer for the Detroit *Free Press* made much of a deal about Homer’s unavailability for an interview following the game. The team had managed to downplay Bull’s tirade in the clubhouse. So, all-in-all, publicity damage was minimized.

Next day Homer's name had not been listed as designated hitter at game time. Hank had arranged for him to arrive at the stadium late, after Bull and the team had taken the field for pre-game warm up.

Homer sat moping, at the farthest end of the bench from Bull, for the first eight innings. It was easy not to have eye contact. His main concern was how to keep a safe distance after the game.

With the game tied at 6 all, going into the top of the ninth, the first two Flags' hitters struck out. Then Broadway Bill – they called him that because he'd grown up in New York City, had taken voice lessons, and delighted in bellowing out scores from Broadway musicals in the clubhouse – the first baseman, got on with a Texas league single.

Bull may have been a powder keg, but he didn't let it affect his baseball decisions. Pokey Washington, Homer's replacement designated hitter, had gone hitless in four times at bat. As Broadway Bill had headed for the on-deck circle prior to his turn at bat, Hank had notified Homer, "You're next." It had taken Homer a moment to register the news. And several moments to pondering the safety of passing by that close to Bull en-route to the on-deck circle. But when the time came, he had to move – quickly – and safely. He made it.

The first three pitches were way outside and the count was quickly at 3 and 0. Now with Homer so dangerous with the bat, and so inept a base runner, it would normally have been a no-brainer for the Lemons to just walk him. But it would have put runners on first and second. They decided to pitch to him. And it was a beautiful pitch – a breaking curve ball just below the belt over the inside corner.

But it was also a beautiful hit. Homer had blasted that ball, hitting the top of the right centerfield wall in such a way that, instead of bouncing back into the field of play, it dribbled its way down into a corner where two sections of the wall meet. "Incredible!" was all Ralph Cambridge, the voice of the Flags, could utter to the fans listening back in Baltimore. "How the hell could he hit that pitch, that far, in that direction?" grumbled the Lemons' pitching coach.

Actually, that was not where he was supposed to have hit it. But who cared? At least in the Flags' dugout, nobody cared. It was an inside-the-park home run! Except that, even after some fumbling by the Lemons' centerfielder followed by a bobbled relay, Homer barely made it to third base without being picked off. Bull was livid. Hank restrained him. The next Flags' batter struck out, and the top half of the inning ended with the Flags up by a run.

Bull managed to restrain himself as the reliever took his warm-up pitches. Thank heavens, for Homer's sake, the Lemons went down one, two, three; and the inning – and the game – ended: Flags 7, Lemons 6.

In spite of Baltimore's three and one record on this opening road trip, Homer was a bit sullen that evening on the flight back to BWI. Juan tried to console him with the reminder that Homer was batting .1000, so far – at least after four games. Well, maybe after just two games in Homer's case. This was a minor fact the Baltimore sports reporters overlooked, understandably, next morning in their excitement of welcoming the team home.

## CHAPTER FOUR

# *Wilmington – Mid April*

Tuesday morning I had to go catch the city bus down on Chester Street in front of the corner grocery to go check in with the Disability Insurance office.

The only other people at the bus stop were a large, fat grumpy woman carrying a baby and dragging about a three-year old behind her. She struggled up onto the bus ahead of me. About half of the seats on the bus were taken, and I wound up sitting almost directly facing her on the opposite side of the bus.

From where we were on-back, all the seats were facing the front of the bus. In the first two rows back to my right were four or five, I'd say, middle school girls making a pain-in-the-ass of themselves. They'd stare at me, then start whispering to each other, then giggle like hell. Little bitches.

Suddenly the fat grumpy mother across from me jerked the living hell out of the three-year old. The kid let out a soft shriek and started sobbing uncontrollably. I thought she'd pulled the kid's whole damned shoulder apart. The kid tried to bury her face in her mother's lap as her sobbing tapered off a little bit, but her mother just shoved her back into her own seat and peered straight ahead with a dull look on her face. The kid leaned her face against the opposite seat back cushion and kept on quietly sobbing.

"15th Street." The bus stopped to let some passengers off and on. I had to get off at 10th, then walk three blocks to a government building. The five dumb-ass young girls had gotten off a stop before that. Thank God.

Actually, it was kind of good to get out and walk past the downtown area. People, busy people, people just out for a walk, young, old, all ages and kinds. But civilized people. Not like the creeps in my building.

"I need to get out more."

The Disability Insurance office was on the third floor. The woman on the elevator looked a little too much like Arsha and Bibbie's mother. Stoneface, ready to explode.

A slow-moving, overweight, uniformed security guard handed me a form to fill out, pointing me to a waiting area to sit until my name was called.

The Disability Insurance people behind the counter were interviewing people to process their claims. They looked like they were trying to be as helpful as possible.

Ten minutes or so I was called to the counter. A Mrs. Pedro was patient and helpful as it was my first actual visit. She took my form, tapped a few things into her computer, and explained that everything was okay and that my check would be mailed to my new address within the next two weeks.

A rickety old pickup burned rubber at the traffic light as I was getting myself off the bus across Chester Street from the grocery at the end of my street.

I needed to stop at the grocery for some things. As I was crossing the street, I almost changed my mind when I saw Arsha and the friend she had played with most every day go into the grocery. What the hell. How can I let those two little bitches get under my skin like that?

I took a shopping basket and headed for the back aisle where it looked like the ice cream and dairy products were. The grocer nodded as I passed the register. Seemed to have a friendly expression on his face. Actually the store looked like an old time grocery. Kind of nice. Not many of them around with all the 7-11's and other modern chain convenience stores.

As I turned left into the dairy products aisle, I saw Arsha and her friend at the other end. They were comparing different candy bars. I paused for a moment, hoping they wouldn't see me. Arsha's friend suddenly slipped a candy bar into her blouse so that it would be held in that loose area where the blouse tucked into her blue jeans. Her cotton blouse was a solid lavender and the grocer wouldn't be able to see the candy bar hidden there.

Rotten little bitch. I almost turned back to the register to let the grocer know what happened. But then I hesitated. Christ, I have enough hassle with Arsha. God knows what kind of crap I'd have to put up with if she was pissed at me for squealing on her friend.

"Joe! What the hell are you doing?" I said to myself. "Letting some damned eight-year olds get to you like that."

I turned and headed back the opposite aisle, hoping they hadn't seen me. A couple other customers came into the store while I was back picking out a loaf of bread. Meantime, I heard the grocer ring up a sale on the register. Must have been Arsha and her friend. Thieving little brats must have paid for something. At least as a cover up. I could see their heads out the store window as they turned the corner to go up our street.

I filled up my basket with enough to get me through a couple of days.

"That will be $19.57."

As he made change I still felt like telling him what I had seen. But I didn't.

My thoughts were racing all over as I walked outside the grocery and headed around the corner. Wonder what makes kids steal like that? Probably saw her mother do it. Maybe even shoplifting in a clothing store. Maybe every damned kid in the neighborhood steals. They all did in Philly, at least where I lived. Most of them did. Wonder how small stores like that stay in business?

Actually I hadn't seen Arsha take anything. Just her friend. But Arsha probably did too. I just hadn't seen her. I shoulda reported it to the grocer when it happened. Well, I hadn't. I sure as hell will next time.

Damned leg. Gonna take me half an hour to go half a block. I could see that nobody was on the front steps as I got closer to the apartment building. Good. Hallelujah. Don't know what I'd say to them right now.

As I was about halfway up there, a couple of boys came down the sidewalk, other side of the street. Damn! They look - - - ; naw, kids that age all look alike.

Sure as hell! Arsha and her friend had appeared b-s'ing up there next to the stoop. I swore a bit as I stumbled slightly over a chink in the old sidewalk. Arsha had turned and looked like she was yelling something back and forth to someone at the second floor window – her mother, I guess. By the time I had limped the rest of the way up the sidewalk, she had disappeared into the building. Her thieving little friend bitch was there waiting by herself as I got to the steps. I avoided looking at her, but I was tired as hell after the trip to Disability Insurance and the stop at the grocery, so I decided to sit for a moment on the stoop before struggling upstairs. I wished she'd just bug-off.

For once I was slightly relieved when Arsha came stumbling back through the front door with Bibbie in-arm. She groaned and grunted and scolded him softly as she put him down.

The stoop was just a heavily worn three-foot by six-foot slab of concrete with three concrete steps leading down to the sidewalk. I had always sat over to one side so as to be out of the way if anybody came out the door. Even so, as soon as Bibbie was standing, he wobbled over against my shoulder, then grabbed my shirt sleeve for dear life so as not to topple over. I don't know if I was too tired to get annoyed or if I was beginning to just give-in. Anyway, it didn't seem to bother me like it would have a few days earlier. And Arsha had immediately jumped down the steps to babble with her friend. So she paid no attention.

Bibbie sort of spun half-way around and sat right up against me on the next step down. He held on to my pant leg for some time just looking around for what happens next. His mother had probably had Arsha bring him down just to get rid of him for a while. I wondered if Dack was up there. There wasn't any noise -- thank God.

I guess I'd begun to soften a little bit. Actually, in a way, he was sort of a cute little guy. Chubby cheeks, and a scared looking little grin once in a while.

He began slowly working his way down the other two steps to find something to play with I guess. He did. It was some grubby-looking old rag of some kind. And after looking it over several times he put it up to his mouth and began chewing it.

"Stop that, Bibbie!" Arsha had darted across from the curb – where she and her friend had been making thumb marks on the hood of a parked car – and grabbed the rag out of his mouth.

"Bibbie!" she screamed, scolding him. "You're not allowed to put dirty stuff in your mouth! You know better!"

I didn't think he did.

"Momma would beat you if she saw that!"

Bibbie screwed up his face and whimpered for a little bit. Then looked around for something else while Arsha threw the rag out onto the street and went back to her friend – probably to plot their next shoplifting act.

"Christ," I muttered to myself. "I forgot, I've got ice cream in that bag! Damn stuff is probably half melted by now." It was.

I managed to slowly get up and drag myself and the grocery bag up the stairs to the third floor. "Damned, rickety old door lock."

I quickly scraped what was left of the ice cream into a bowl and ate about half of it, before washing the rest down the drain. "Goddamn kids caused me to forget what I was doing."

"I've got to talk to the landlady about that lock next time she stops by. At least it is quiet here. Don't ever hear that much racket from their apartment, which is right below. Just the normal stuff. A shout once in a while – usually sounds like their mother. But that's normal. Nothing real bad."

"She, or maybe Dack, plays that damned rock a little loud sometimes. But not real often. This sure as hell beats that zoo I lived in Philly. It was dirty, it was loud, and what a shit-awful band of teenagers.

Drugs and everything with it. At least there aren't any teenagers I've seen around here. Damn! And by the time Arsha's a teenager, they'll be long gone somewhere. Or I will be."

"Why can't they just ship kids off to Greenland, or somewhere and bring them back when they've grown up? Problem is I need some human to talk to. It was okay at work. Guys were okay. Had a good time. Then the accident. Then the miserable recovery. Then Becky takes off on me. I was glad to get this place. Even though she had zipped along again. Before I even got here."

"But it's peaceful. But damnit, I don't have anybody to talk to but those two brats. Sure as hell don't want to talk to their mother bitch – and sure as hell not Dack! And not that creepy bastard on the first floor. Only seen him a couple of times. Never around much. He looks like a wart. So what have I got for fun? Arsha and Bibbie. Can't drive. Hard to hobble anywhere. And don't know where to hobble around here anyway. Shit."

"Seems that nobody in the next door buildings ever hang around much. Hardly see them. They just seem to go to work and go back to their apartments and never talk to anybody. 'Course I can understand why they wouldn't bother talking to anybody in this building."

"Don't even seem to be any retired people around. But it's peaceful. Mostly."

"Wonder what the hell those two brats do all weekend in their apartment when they're not out front? Their mother seems to come and go and must just leave them there alone. Wonder what she did with Bibbie when Arsha was in school? And why the hell do I bother? I must be losing it. I gotta get out and around more. Meet some people."

* * * *

Bibbie was out on the grass strip whacking a stick at the front end of a parked car when I got down to the stoop next day. Arsha wasn't around. I wondered why the hell he was down there alone.

"Bibbie! Get over here."

"Stop that!" I called.

He paused a moment – glanced over at me – gave the car a couple more whacks, then wriggling his arms and doing a little dance he turned 'round toward the stoop and began beating his stick at the air. All the while he was jabbering some sort of a giggle. Most I'd heard him say since I moved in.

About that time Arsha came out the door. Kind of quiet. We didn't say anything to each other. She went down and took Bibbie by the arm and brought him back over by the stoop. I could tell she was thinking about something as she sat down on the lower step looking out at the street. At least she wasn't pestering me.

"Mister."

I didn't respond.

"Mister, Momma said to ask you if you could take Bibbie and me to the park."

"Well, Momma can go to hell," I said to myself.

"She was s'pposed to take us today, but she's too busy and she said to ask you."

"I'm too busy too."

"What'r you busy at?"

I was wondering what park she was talking about. Where was it and can't they see I don't have a car and can't walk very well. "What the hell is with Arsha and her dumb bitch Momma?"

I never answered her. She kept pestering the hell out of me for another five minutes or so until I finally gave her a hard, blunt "no!" She shut up for a little bit.

She finally stood up, took Bibbie by the arm – babbling and waving his stick, and all – and started slowly walking him up the sidewalk. I didn't say anything.

After about ten yards or so, she paused – Bibbie couldn't move very fast anyway. "Guess where we're goin', Mister." She turned and looked at me with a smart-ass little nose in the air. I didn't answer. And I didn't give a shit.

"We're goin' to the park. If you won't take us, we'll just go anyway. C'mon Bibbie, can't you go faster than that?" she scolded; finally picking him up with a struggle. He was a load for her, and I figured they wouldn't get far.

But between putting him down and making him walk, and half-carrying, half-dragging, she managed to get about three buildings up the street to where I couldn't really see them any more. And not that I gave a damn, but I got up and moved down to the sidewalk to see where they were.

They had turned off to the right and disappeared.

"Christ, what if they get into trouble – or something happens to them? I'll probably get blamed. That goddamn mother is nuts, and who knows what the hell she might do."

As it turned out, where they had turned was a narrow alley-way leading all the way through past the row of houses backing up to our building and into that next street.

Arsha and Bibbie had just made it past the cross-alley that ran along mid-way to that street. Even at my pace I should be able to catch up with them by the time they get there, I'm thinking to myself.

Bibbie was slowly trundling along with his chubby little legs hesitating every other step. Arsha had him by the hand and would look down at him, coaxing and tugging. She hadn't looked back at me catching up with them, and I wasn't going to yell unless they got dangerously close to that street. But I hurried it up as much as I could when a delivery truck, followed by an old model black sedan, went zipping by. Up to then I couldn't see what was on the other side of the street because of all the trees.

When I was about 20 feet behind them Arsha stopped to pick Bibbie up and she saw me coming. She didn't say anything. But she paused. She was probably getting tired of fooling with him and hoped I was coming to help – *not* to make them go back home.

By the time I caught them, I could see the large park running along the other side of the street at least two blocks in each direction and as far as I could see into it straight ahead.

"Mister, would you just help me with Bibbie a little bit? He's a pain," she whined hopefully.

What the hell. I had come after them to make them go back home. But it would be a shame, after they made it this far, not to let them at least cross over to the park for a little bit. Besides, I kinda wondered what all was in that park. Might be an interesting place I could go to, to sit during the day time. Might meet someone to talk to there from time to time. And get the hell away from that damned front stoop.

Before I knew what I was doing I had picked the little bastard up. Immediately, he started wriggling, I have to say, almost with glee. Kicking his little legs, waving his little toddler arms, and patting me once or twice on top of the head. He even giggled, which I hadn't seen him do much before. Arsha almost froze in place – looking mildly surprised and mildly happy.

"Okay, damn it, we'll go to the park for just a few minutes."

"What the hell have I gotten into?" I muttered to myself.

Arsha was happy for any small victory and quickly started leading us to the edge of the street, looking both ways for cars. At least her mother had taught her that. Or somebody had.

I put Bibbie down as soon as we got across the street and into the grassy edge of the park. What a beautiful park. Trees as far as I could see. And way off to the right a large open area with ball fields. And beyond that, about 45 degrees off to our right, it looked like a playground area with swings and teeter totters and jungle-gym, or whatever they called those newer versions.

Ahead to the left it looked like the park sloped down, but because of all the trees I couldn't see to what. Later I learned it went down to a little stream and beyond the stream to the distant left was a small zoo for kids.

Arsha had spotted the playground area and headed straight that direction, pausing to make sure we were following. That was fine by me. After all, if I could get these two busy at the playground, they'd probably be less of a pain in the ass than anywhere else.

"Go ahead," I told her. "We'll catch up."

Bibbie had bent over to pick something out of the grass. I didn't rush him. I was getting a little tired by then. Let him keep himself busy. He looked up at me, babbling for some attention to whatever he had found. It was some kind of a worm, and he was having trouble picking it up. I picked him up instead of the worm and headed for the playground.

Arsha had already made it almost to the swing set area, and we still had 100 yards to catch up with her.

I don't think Bibbie had ever seen a teeter totter before. I wondered if he'd ever seen a playground. I had first set him down next to the down end of the teeter totter. But no sooner had he started grabbing it than some brat, seven or eight years old, had come over and abruptly pulled the other end down, barely missing Bibbie's face as the end he was holding went zipping up. I just glared at the kid, then took Bibbie by the hand and led him toward the jungle-gym.

Meanwhile, Arsha was swinging – had pumped her swing up to about as high as she could. There were a dozen or so kids, and a half-dozen moms busy at the various equipment. Bibbie was the youngest one at the jungle-gym. I let him crawl up to a flexible plastic walkway about my chest level. The little bastard was absolutely thrilled. A couple bigger brats almost knocked him off as they went scrambling by to go down a tubular slide that Bibbie hadn't spotted yet. But he was bug-eyed as he watched them screaming and giggling go down the chute, then hurry back around to a set of steps that led directly up to the top of the slide, to go down it again.

By the time they had started their third trip, Bibbie had edged himself over to the mouth of the tube and was looking at me with big joy and excitement, wanting me to help him go down. What the hell. It looked safe enough. So I helped him cautiously get himself into a starting position. He was a little anxious, and I had to tell the other two brats to wait a minute until I could get around to the bottom of the slide to let him know I was there to catch him when he came down.

I had to coax him a little. The other two were getting antsy. I finally had to go over and hold onto his little rib area on both sides, then slowly nudge him on until his own weight took him sliding all six feet or so down. He was surprised enough when he got to the bottom, and I had had time to get around to him before he began letting me know he would like to do it again.

I let him go one more time, but battling the other two brats for another turn was a pain in the ass, at the rate I was able to maneuver around.

I had noticed that Arsha was now pushing some other kid on the swings; thank God she had found a friend, saving me some hassle. Nevertheless, I might be able to get Bibbie away from the jungle-gym by showing him what Arsha was up to.

He fussed like hell when I picked him up to head over toward the swings. Oh shit! He had peed his pants and got my chest and shoulder all soaked. Damn it! Luckily, when he saw Arsha he started pointing and giggling so it was easy to put him down and let him toddle his own way over. It took awhile. I'm not sure Arsha was all that happy to see us. So I spotted a park bench nearby and tugged Bibbie over there while I sat down for a rest. It was a struggle, but as Arsha paid no attention to us I finally got him busy playing with an old chunk of broken rope laying there by the bench while I rested awhile.

"What a great spot. If I could just come over here without these two. I'd come here every day."

A young couple with a dog came by. It was a friendly pooch. Went straight toward Bibbie. The couple smiled and said good morning and asked if that was okay (for the dog to go close to Bibbie). "Fine, if he's friendly," I said.

Bibbie was fascinated. He tried to pet, or whack was more like it, with his chubby little hands and arms and unsuccessfully reached for the wagging tail a couple of times. The dog licked his face and that did it. Bibbie backed off, not sure what that was all about.

The couple smiled and I smiled back and off they went, slowly tugging the dog to get moving. Bibbie watched them for a moment, but was soon back to playing with his rope toy.

"Arsha, you about ready to go?" I called.

She wasn't – but we went anyway.

## CHAPTER FIVE

# *Baltimore – Mid April*

In spite of Homer's limited and disastrous earlier experiences, it was great to be finally back in hallowed Ripkin Field. Even Bull was upbeat late that next afternoon as everybody filtered into the clubhouse, a little earlier than usual.

But in spite of the extraordinarily positive vibes offered by the Baltimore media, fan turnout for opening game was a bit light. After all, although the Flags were solidly in second place in their division right then, they had finished in last, or next to last place, the last several seasons in a row.

Fortunately, the weather was mild that evening. The opening ceremonies were stirring. And Homer was totally impressed with the massive fireworks display coordinated with a duplicate display from some old fort somewhere out in Baltimore's inner-harbor.

Most of the Atlanta Confederates were wearing Confederate caps during pre-game warm-up, and Bull had noticed. He had filed a protest, and although the Atlanta manager had explained that they would all be wearing regulation baseball caps by game time – after significant scurrying around – all were quickly changed to Bull's satisfaction. And in spite of the Confederate flag arm patches on their sleeves, the game was allowed to begin.

"Play ball!" the umpire bellowed. After a brief roar from the small crowd of four thousand fans the opening home game of the season commenced.

In Homer's first at-bat, in the second inning, he singled into center field, scoring a runner from second. The fans had heard some about this unusual rookie and gave him an enthusiastic round of applause. Baltimore's 1 to 0 lead held until the fourth inning when Homer again singled, this time with two men on. The runner scored from third and the Flags were up 2 to 0.

As Homer jogged back to the dugout following the Flags' third out a couple of his teammates called encouraging remarks as they passed him en-route to their fielding positions for the top of the fifth inning. Hank met him at the dugout with an enthusiastic pat on the back. Hank had done that after each hit Homer had gotten in this young season. "Hank's a good guy," Homer thought to himself. Thank goodness for Hank.

Bull remained stolid, frozen in his tracks at the home-plate end of the dugout, eyes directed straight at the pitcher's mound.

Bottom of the sixth, one out and bases loaded; Homer stepped into the batter's box. The Confederates' catcher muttered some choice words at Homer. Foul ball into the stands behind first. Next pitch, ninety-one mile per hour fast ball, right down the middle. The Confederate pitcher was swearing the moment the ball left his finger tips. All three base-runners scored, and Homer made it all the way to third base on the booming three run triple, putting the Flags up 5 to 0. After a

Confederates pitching change, the next two Flags batters popped up, and the inning ended with the game well in hand.

Except that the top of the eighth ended in near disaster. After two pitching changes by the Flags, they managed to escape the top half of the inning with a one run lead as the Confederates had put four big ones on the scoreboard.

With Baltimore leading 5 to 4 in the bottom of the eighth, Homer took his practice swings and stepped into the box to the cordial welcome of the Confederate's catcher. The Confederate's catcher and pitcher had been given the word, "Do not let this guy get another hit!" "Walk him if you must, but no hit!"

But after all, with nobody on, let's at least test him they decided. So although they didn't throw Homer any good pitches, they were just good enough to be tempting. First pitch, fouled back into the press box. Next pitch, "ball one." Then two more long foul balls down into the left-field stands, followed by a high, inside fastball which Homer just managed to duck, falling hard into the chalk and dust at the plate. He brushed himself off, glared at the pitcher – although Homer wasn't very good at glaring – and awaited the next pitch.

Six foul balls later – one which his Father almost caught behind the Flags' dugout – with the count at three and two, the Confederate catcher called a seemingly endless time-out for a conference on the mound. Homer figured they were going to either hit him or walk him. But they didn't. The "dumb bastards" (according to Atlanta's manager) threw Homer a hittable pitch. Homer only got a single out of it. But the grounder he hit was so hard that as it skimmed over the mound it nearly bit the Confederate pitcher's ankle, sending him tumbling into the dust. It so rattled him that the Flags' next batter zipped the first pitch into right field, which might have turned into a double had Homer been able to get past second base.

Jose was next up, and he hammered a long, high fly ball into right-center. To the Confederate center fielder that ball seemed to take forever to get to him. Could he prevent two runs from scoring? He heaved a near perfect throw to the shortstop who fired a near perfect relay home. And to the astonishment of everyone in the ballpark, especially to Bull, Homer was tagged out as he finally arrived at home plate.

Bull's reaction cannot be repeated in print. And unfortunately, the next two batters went down swinging. So the eighth inning ended with the score: Baltimore 5, Atlanta 4.

Fortunately, for the Flags (and maybe even for Homer), Bart Berkeley, Baltimore's "reliable as an old shoe" reliever, took the Confederates down in order in the top of the ninth, and the Baltimore Flags moved into a first place tie in their division.

Next morning the headlines in the Baltimore Sun sports page read "Hom(er) Opener, Near Disaster." One writer suggested sending Homer down to the rookie league for a couple of months. Another was more generous, as an afterthought, mentioning Homer's five RBI's in the first home opener that the Flags had won "since Francis Scott Key wrote the National Anthem here." And in closing he had noted the enigma of Homer's batting average, still at 1000.

Bull had spared Homer's life back in the clubhouse following the game. Bull was even slightly pleased at squeaking out a home opener victory. But Hank took no chances. He had cajoled Homer into quickly showering, dressing and getting the devil out of there "so you can go have dinner with your parents in one piece." Homer obliged and treated his Mom and Dad to a big spread at Dan's Big Dog that evening. His parents had asked his brother, Joe, to come down by train from Wilmington that evening for the festivities, but had gotten a flat-out "No!"

By sheer coincidence Baltimore won again the following evening by a score of 5 to 4 in their second and concluding game of the series against the Confederates. But this time it was by way of a dramatic comeback in the bottom of the ninth. The Confederates had gone ahead 4 to 0 in the top of the first and had held that lead for eight and a half innings. They had wisely walked Homer his first four times at bat.

The first man up in the bottom of the ninth had struck out; all the fans had gone home. That was the signal for Arley Lancaster, Baltimore's next batter, to whack a bases-empty homer over the right field wall – Atlanta 4, Baltimore 1 – one out, nobody on; next man up singled. Then two consecutive walks, and the bases were loaded with Homer coming to bat.

With a 4 to 1 lead, that was no big problem for the Confederates. They'd simply walk Homer, give up a run, and get the next man out. But they didn't. Homer sent the first pitch, which had not been quite far enough outside, soaring out of Ripkin Field and landing in the beef barbecue vendor's cart, shutting him down for the evening.

Homer's grand-slam had given the Flags a two game sweep of Atlanta, leaving Baltimore at five and one early in the season. Headline on the Sun's sports page next morning poked fun at Baltimore's "Give up" fans who had left the game at the beginning of the ninth inning: "Missed it, didn't ya."

Bull had been around baseball a long time. To him Homer's hitting streak was no doubt just luck – dumb luck in Homer's case. And it would all probably go into a disastrous reversal real soon. In fact, the morning of that second Atlanta game he had made a plea to the Flag's general manager, with a brash forcefulness only Bull could muster, to "Get Homer the hell outa' here and down to the minors where he belongs!"

But the G.M. wasn't buying it. He was beginning to smell blood. Not just in winning ball games, but in getting some fans back into the ballpark. Next morning his hunch was vindicated by the local media. Not only had the Sun and the local TV reporters turned Homer into an overnight celebrity but so had ESPN, The Daily News, and media across the country. Next issue of Sports Illustrated featured Homer in a "Baseball Revived in Baltimore?" article on page 25.

Bull crossed his fingers; and cursed.

## CHAPTER SIX

# *Wilmington – Mid April*

The walk home took awhile. Arsha carried Bibbie about ten feet of it. I carried him about three-quarters of the way, and he toddled the rest.

I don't know why I bothered to ask about things. I guess because I hadn't had anybody to talk to for awhile, and I just wanted to talk to someone.

"How long have you lived here, Arsha?"

It took her awhile to answer. She was doing a couple of her hopscotch routines on the sidewalk while we were waiting for some traffic to pass before we could cross the street to head up the alley.

"A year," she answered. Then she looked quickly that traffic had passed and ran across the street ahead of us.

"Where does your mother work?"

We had caught up with her.

"At the cafeteria."

She wasn't paying much attention to my questions. She looked like she had her mind on other things as she brushed at the hedges every few feet along the alley.

"In the daytime you mean?" It was none of my damned business what her mother did, but I'd always kind of wondered why she was in and out at all different times. And I did wonder who took care of Arsha and Bibbie when she wasn't there. Not that SOB Dack, I hoped.

I had just put Bibbie down to toddle on his own for a little bit when two brats came tearing up behind us on bikes. They went zipping by so close that one of them brushed Arsha's arm. She yelled at them, but they were long gone.

"At the cafeteria?" Why was I bothering with this? It took her a moment to get back on track with me.

"Just part-time," she finally answered.

"*Bitch* probably just mops the floors or carries out the trash," I thought to myself.

"She brings us some yummy things a lot. She brought us some cookies and chocolate brownies once."

"*Bitch* probably steals it all," I figured.

As we rounded the corner onto our street, I could see some older woman going into our building. By the time we made it down the sidewalk to our front stoop, she was coming back out. I realized she was Mrs. Kline, the landlady. I had only actually seen her once before. "She's probably here to collect somebody's rent, " I thought to myself. "The *bitch* probably hasn't paid this month. Or maybe the weird-looking bastard on the first floor." We were the only three apartments in the building.

She gave us a quick hello. "Is your mother here today?" she asked Arsha.

"I don't know where she is," Arsha said, looking half scared to answer.

Mrs. Kline shrugged, looked frustrated, and glanced over at me. "She's always late. She'll pay it eventually, but she's forever late. Not bad enough to evict her – she'll pay the rent sometime. R'rrr!" Mrs. Kline shrugged again and rolled her eyes.

Arsha had eased away to do her hopscotch a little further down the sidewalk than usual. Bibbie was sitting on the bottom step playing with a small concrete chip he'd found there. Mrs. Kline had paused and just looked at him, sort of carefully, for quite a while.

"He looks okay today," she finally said. I couldn't tell if she was talking to me or to herself.

Then she looked directly at me with kind of a half-glare and half-frown, "Last time I was here he had bruises all over him." She paused and then went on. "But the worst time was once last fall. I was headed up the stairs to their apartment. To try to collect the rent, you know. Well, their apartment door was open —and suddenly I heard this blood curdling screaming along with some thudding. By that time I could see right in and here was that woman beating this child with a pan. She looked half crazy. Soon as she saw me she stopped, grabbed him up, and disappeared into the bedroom. Next I hear this terrible thump, as though she had just thrown him hard as possible down on a bed. She then came charging back out, again just looking half-crazy. Frankly, I was scared. I didn't know what she might do next. Only thing I could hear from the bedroom was a little gasping and sobbing. At least he wasn't unconscious I thought. Anyway, she just stared at me for a moment and then told me she couldn't pay me until next week. At that, I just left."

Mrs. Kline just kept looking directly at me. Sort of trembling a little bit. I didn't know if she expected me to say something or not, but she just kept looking at me.

"I guess maybe I should have reported the incident to the social welfare – or to somebody – but I didn't," she pondered. Then she just stared across the street for a little bit, then left.

## CHAPTER SEVEN

# *Baltimore - Late April*

The next three games in Baltimore's opening home stand were against the archrival Washington Bureaucrats.

As things had turned out this was to be Washington's season opener. The Bureaucrats had been scheduled to open their season at home their first five games, followed by two games at New York prior to visiting Baltimore. But due to delays in regulatory approvals of the new seats in their stadium and of the team's new uniforms, they had not been able to play yet in Washington. It seems that five different Federal agencies had discovered critical issues requiring approval, but that the processing of the information had gotten bogged down by various computer systems and all was a mess. Poor Bureaucrats. Then they had been rained out both games in New York.

Fortunately for Baltimore, this all reflected in Washington's play that "opening" game against the Flags. They were terrible: seven errors, no hits, six pitchers – all chased from the mound by Baltimore hitting – and a very frustrated, and eventually ejected from the game, manager.

From the Baltimore perspective, it was beautiful. Ripkin Field was jammed. First sellout in nearly a decade. The fans were responding.

The Flags were in first place and Homer had become a marvelous curiosity, not just in Baltimore, but in baseball lore around the nation. Here was this teenager, nearly useless at anything other than at batting; batting 1000! At least after seven games. But the Baltimore fans were so starved for excitement, it hadn't taken much. And as the local sports reporter reminded everybody, each game the Flags had won had been won by Homer's hitting.

The media had been just as starved as the fans. And they responded with bursts of exaggerated enthusiasm.

Luckily for everybody involved, Homer was not at all spoiled by all the attention. He really hadn't grasped it all yet. To Homer he wasn't doing anything much different than he'd done in that batting practice cage back in Marietta those couple of years. And indeed, he wasn't.

Homer didn't know whether Washington was thirty miles away or 300 miles away, so the extra attention to the Bureaucrats as almost crosstown rivals was lost on him. About all Homer knew was to get up to the plate and hit the ball. He also knew that Bull was always pissed off at him, and that Jose was his best buddy. And Hank was a good guy too, especially when Bull was sizzling.

Homer had been considering all this as he sat poking down at the dugout floor, at his end of the bench, throughout much of the first inning. So when it came his turn to bat he wasn't bothered by whether the Washington pitcher was a leftie or not; nor what kinds of pitches he was throwing. He did glance up at the scoreboard and noticed that the Flags were leading 6 to 0 in the bottom of the first. He also noticed that there were runners on first and second with two out. He took the first pitch low and inside.

Homer rarely bothered to look down at the third base coach for batting signals. He normally wouldn't have remembered what they meant anyway. And even if he had, he didn't know how to adjust his swing based on some coach's hand signal. Hank had worked with him, patiently and fruitlessly. It just hadn't taken. All Homer knew was how to hit the ball; not always where the coach, and Bull, intended, but he hit it.

And he hit it, that second pitch from the beleaguered Washington leftie, skimming the turf hard down over second base, just out of reach of the Bureaucrat shortstop. The runner scored from second base, making it Flags 7, Bureacrats 0. But because of where Homer had placed, or not placed, his hit, the runner from first had to hold up at second.

In frustration, Bull had recently begun keeping track of the number of lost opportunities at advanced extra bases Homer had cost the team with his grossly inept placement of hits. This was number 9 for the season.

The first inning finally ended, the second was uneventful, and the Flags led 10 to 0 as Homer stepped into the batter's box for the bottom of the third.

The first three pitches were wide – count: 3 and 0. Then Homer did something he rarely did. He swung at a bad pitch. He hit it. He hit it very hard – right over third base. This could be the end of Homer's perfect batting average – almost. But the left fielder was way out of position, and by the time he retrieved the ball, even at Homer's turtle grade speed, he touched first base just ahead of the throw to first.

On base by a hair – no damage done to the batting average. Homer even scored as the next Flag batter sent one booming over the center field wall for a two-run home run.

The game atmosphere turned into a carnival, especially in the stands. The beer vendors were happy that the game seemed to take forever. The Flags went on to capture a 17 to 0 victory over the Bureaucrats. Homer finished the game with two hits and three walks.

That evening one Baltimore TV station even suggested a looming World Series (with only 154 games to go).

The town was giddy. And it got giddier as the Flags polished off the Bureaucrats the following evening 5 to 3. With the score tied at 3, as Homer went to the plate for the bottom of the eighth, he hammered a double to right center scoring two runners. The Flags reliever put the Bureaucrats down 1-2-3 in the top of the ninth. And, well, you'd have thought Baltimore had just won the World Series.

Next evening though, the third and final game of this home stand against the Bureaucrats, things got bizarre. Homer was intentionally walked his first three times at bat. Then, in the bottom of the seventh, with Baltimore leading 4 to 3, the Washington pitcher walked the first two Flags at bat. Up came Homer. You can never explain how these things can happen to pitchers but baseball is a crazy game. Instead of loading the bases with an intentional walk, as one might have expected, they unloaded the bases as Homer powered a 3 run home run over the left field wall.

Then things got interesting. With Baltimore holding a 7 to 3 lead going into the top of the ninth, Bull had gotten a sudden pain in his gut and decided he'd best go into the clubhouse with the team physician, leaving things in Hank's hands. After all, the game was well in hand. At the same moment, Bo Monica, the Flags center fielder, reported that he'd injured his hand sliding into second base, and that he'd better not take the field in the bottom of the ninth. Now this left Hank in a dilemma. Eddie York, who would normally fill in at center field, had been called to the hospital where his wife was in labor, about to deliver. And Mack Hatten, the only other reasonable replacement, had been used as a pinch hitter for the starting pitcher earlier in the game. What a clever move that had been.

Now Hank, with a quick decision to make, had a momentary lapse of sanity, decided to put Homer in center field for their final inning. "What the hell. We got this one anyway. And how much damage could he do in one inning?" Bull answered that question later in the clubhouse.

The first Bureaucrat up hit a lazy blooper out over second base. It would be a routine single. Except that as Homer ran up to field it, the ball went right between his legs. By the time Pedro Antonio, the right fielder -- who had moved over to back Homer up – could field the ball and get it to third, the runner was already there. This had been Homer's first defensive play opportunity of the season so his error percentage was also 1000 (in baseball math).

Next Bureaucrat up slapped a very hard to handle ground ball down between first and second. The ball was momentarily bobbled, allowing the run to score and leaving a man on first. Flags 7 to Bureaucrats 4.

The Bureaucrats then sent in a pinch hitter who started off with four straight foul balls into the stands followed by two low and inside called balls, followed by three more foul balls, then by a conference on the mound. Homer meantime, getting bored with all this, decided to respond to some avid fans in the center field stands who were shouting great words of encouragement to him. Thus, he totally missed the next pitch which, fortunately for him, went fair down the third base line for a single, leaving Bureaucrats on first and third.

Homer continued his shouting discussion with the fans while a new pitcher came in and went through his warm ups. More and more fans joined in the center field discussion with Homer while the next Washington batter was given a base-on-balls, loading the bases.

So just as the following Washington batter connected with the first pitch for a high fly ball to deep center, Homer was in the midst of responding to a fan's question, "What's your favorite beer, Homer?"

At the last moment some of the fans tried to alert Homer to the impending crisis. Just as he turned around the ball hit the turf nearby, bouncing into the wall, then dribbling the opposite direction Homer had expected. By the time he finally managed to hunt it down, two runs had scored with the third enroute from third base. The hitter was headed for third when Homer's throw bounced into the ball girl down the third base line. The fourth run scored. Washington 8, Baltimore 7 – Homer two errors.

As the next five batters (2 Washington, 3 Baltimore) went down in order, Hank stood stunned at his lonely end of the dugout.

Homer had hung around til the final Flag teammate had exited into the clubhouse before he tried to sneak in unnoticed.

The physician administering to Bull in the clubhouse had concluded that Bull's pains were nothing more than excessive gas, which was relieved by a routine procedure just before the game ended.

But the physician's problems were only beginning. When Bull was apprised of the events of the ninth inning, he responded as any overweight Type A might. After giving him a heavy does of sedatives, they removed him by ambulance.

When the Flags' G.M. and key staff visited the hospital the following morning, Bull charged out of bed waving his fists and bellowing that this time they were to banish Homer to the lowest level minor league club in existence, hopefully not in the U.S., "and by God Hank should be sent with him!" Quickly realizing what he had done, he helped the nurse back to her feet, charged back into bed, and stuck out his lower lip. Then when he didn't get an immediate response from his astounded guests, he started shouting orders at everyone, including the physician, who promptly administered another dose of heavy sedative and asked the G.M. and his party to "come back tomorrow."

Back in the clubhouse after the game the previous evening all was sullen. Homer was mildly surprised, and greatly relieved, that he was not accosted by any of his teammates. After the others had all departed, Jose slipped down to Homer, whose locker was at the far end of the row against the end wall, and consoled him: "Cheer up, amigo. You're still batting 1000."

The two of them chose to drive up to a quiet bar in nearby Towson for a beer. Jose felt that people were not as volatile in that particular place, and they could wind down there in peace.

"Besides, if you look at the big picture, we did take two out of three from Washington. And we're still tied for first place." Homer appreciated Jose's positive outlook. Now, if Jose only had some influence with Bull.

The local media was all over the place. How could Hank have allowed Homer into center field? Whoever allowed such an idiot as Homer into the major leagues to begin with? Is Bull still alive (in spite of hospital assurances that he was)? And how could the Flags possibly be in first place?

The Washington Post was more gentle, publishing a full page picture – a magnificent piece of photography – capturing the fly ball about 20 feet off the ground as Homer stood there with his back to it while chatting with the fans.

Next morning the Flags headed off for Philadelphia for a three game series with the last place Lawyers. Homer was still with the team – and was even allowed to make the road trip, thanks to a publicity savvy, attendance oriented G.M. who had prevailed in his "discussions" with Bull. But, as a consolation, Homer was to be benched for at least one game.

## CHAPTER EIGHT

# *Wilmington – Late April*

A couple weeks later I decided I'd sneak off to the park alone, while those two weren't around. I had gotten myself hobbled almost up to the alley-way, where I had hoped to disappear when sure as hell I hear Arsha calling after me. Damn! I pretended not to hear at first, but she kept coming.

"Mister, are you going to the park?" about five times. "Can Bibbie and me come with you?"

"Not today."

"Why? Why not? We won't be any bother. I promise. I'll take care of Bibbie. Please. Please, Mister. Please."

She wasn't gonna let up. And she could move faster than me.

I didn't answer. Just kept going, around the corner and into the alley. I was halfway down the alley toward the street running along the park when I could hear them coming.

"Hurry up, Bibbie! Do I have to carry you the whole way? How can we catch up that way?"

I was gonna have to wait for them at the street anyway so I just limped on until I got there.

What a beautiful day it was. Trees in their full spring glory. Lots of shrubs along with rows of spring flowers. Just a light breeze and a great sunny day. It was one of those days you just couldn't help but feel good. Ahead through the trees I could see the swing sets in full gear and a couple softball games in action on those diamonds way off to the right.

Arsha and Bibbie seemed to be coming slower every step. She was probably getting tired toting the little bastard most of the way. They finally caught up.

As we crossed the street and started into the park, some people on bikes passed in front of us on a bike path leading down into the woods on our left. I decided to head off that way just to see what was down that part of the park. Arsha started moaning about wanting to go to the swing sets, but I just ignored her and kept on going. Next thing I know, she heads off alone to the swings, leaving Bibbie by himself about 20 feet behind me. God damn it!

I probably shouldn't have let her go off by herself, without keeping an eye on her. But crap! I hadn't wanted them to follow me in the first place! Bibbie started slowly toddling in her direction. But I'd be damned if she was going to dictate my day in the park.

I tell you, I almost chuckled watching Bibbie from behind, as he went toddling off, falling down every third or fourth step. Chubby little bastard. I finally caught up with him, picked him up and headed the opposite direction down the bike path. He seemed to think it was all funny as he wriggled and giggled and finally got fascinated by a couple of bikes that went peddling slowly past us. About 50 yards or so down, I sat down on a park bench to rest with Bibbie on my lap. At first he got down and toddled around, holding on to the edge of the bench all the time. Then the little bastard decided he wanted back up on my lap. "Oh, for Chrissake." But for whatever reason, I gave in.

I hoped to hell that Arsha was staying out of trouble. Last thing I needed was to have to go lugging after her. For a long time Bibbie just sat there, taking in the scene. A couple of times I started to put him over onto the bench to sit by himself. But he put up such a fuss it was easier just to let him stay on my lap. Then, finally, of course, the little bastard dozed off.

People kept biking by and jogging by and walking by, and there I sat with Bibbie on my lap. A couple of times people, who I guess liked kids, smiled at us as they walked by.

As I sat there figuring when I'd finally have to get up and go look for Arsha – what the hell's going on? These kids aren't my responsibility, son-of-a-bitch – here she comes down the path with some other kid about her same age.

"Mister, Penny wants me to go home with her to her house to play." Then she just looked at me.

Now what the hell was I supposed to say? "Yes," and face the wrath of hell if anything happened? Or "No," and face the whining and bitching for the next half hour?

So I didn't say anything.

Meanwhile, Bibbie woke up and started squirming. I put him over on the bench by himself, and he was okay for the moment.

Then the pestering began. The goddamned pestering! "Huh, Mister? Huh? Is it okay if I go? Huh?"

All of a sudden, an older woman, who had just passed by on her bike, lost control and went falling all over the place a few yards down the path. I jumped up immediately – as best I could jump – and headed down to help. A couple other people had seen her fall and got there just before I did.

Didn't look good. She was conscious but in some pain. A couple of us got the bike gently pulled away from her, and a woman put down a folded-up shirt for her to lay her head on. Somebody had called 911 on their cell phone.

A couple of women – one I think must have been a nurse – seemed to take charge. They tried to comfort the poor woman while we all waited for the emergency van to show up.

"What happened to her, Mister? Is she still alive?"

No, Arsha, you dumb little bitch. She groans and twists her face in pain while she is dead.

"Arsha, where the devil is Bibbie?" I suddenly realized that Bibbie was nowhere in sight. She just stood there and looked stupid. I got worried quickly. "Where the hell is he?" I shouted at her impatiently. She and her friend, Penny, scrambled to look, and I followed limping along.

Now how the little bastard knew to go behind a tree to do his pee pee I couldn't figure. But there he was, doing his deed, pissing half on the tree and half on himself.

"Oh for Chrissakes. Now I've got to carry him home all soaked," I grumbled.

The emergency squad got there pretty quickly. The two paramedics got right to it. They said the woman's arm was broken, but didn't seem to be any other serious injury. They loaded her carefully onto the van and zipped off. Some guy in the small crowd seemed to know where she lived and offered to take her bike back.

As everybody left, Arsha started in on me again.

"You two go back up to the swing sets for now. I'm taking Bibbie on a walk around the path." I pointed to a narrow walking path that looped up through the woods to the right off the bike path. It had to wind past somewhere in sight of the swing set area.

"Well, Mister, …"

"Get!" I barked, and headed up the side of the bike path holding Bibbie's hand. I hoped that Bibbie would toddle a fair bit of the walk. I was in no hurry. And, after all, he'd had a good nap on my lap back there.

I could tell that Arsha and her new friend had paused and watched us for awhile before they slowly turned to head back up to the playground area. Probably trying to figure out whether to obey me or not.

This was a big trip for Bibbie. He saw a chipmunk and tried to go after it. Then he tripped over a stretch of a large tree root growing partway out into the path. I had to brush the grit off his chubby little hands.

Once he started out into the woods to pick a big white blossom off a shrub. He couldn't quite reach it so I plucked it for him, but he had dropped it by the time he got back onto the path, and was on to other things. I shoulda known this couldn't last. He soon wore down and had to be picked up. Soaked shorts or not, I carried him against my right chest and shoulder so he could look back from where we'd come. I was slow plodding, but not all that uncomfortable, as we went on up the path through that relaxing stretch of woods and shrubs and patches of sunlight.

Luckily, Bibbie suddenly saw a squirrel and started kicking and squealing to get down. The squirrel was long gone by the time he got his little legs headed back toward where it had been. And as soon as I got him turned around and headed the right direction, he saw another one coming down a tree up ahead of us.

What a busy guy Bibbie was. He started pointing and looking up at me. As though I was going to catch the squirrel for him. In his rush as the big squirrel hunter, he fell down twice over the next several feet of path. So I picked him up again and off we limped.

Making it up into the playground area, I could see Arsha and friend just sitting on the grass talking. The swing sets were full of other kids. I knew what I was in for, and I wasn't about to put up with any crap. As soon as she saw us, she got up and started up into her bitchy whine routine, which I cut off instantly.

"We're headed home Arsha. Tell your friend you'll catch up with her next time."

* * * *

"Arsha, could you carry Bibbie across the street, here? My leg's bothering me some. I'm not real steady."

"Why do I have to carry him?"

Little bitch was getting whinier every day. Probably getting it from her mother.

"I just told you why. I don't want to take a chance stumblin' in the middle of the street if I'm carrying him. Just pick him up and carry him across the street, damn it!"

She gave a scowl like I'd screwed up her whole day and grabbed him up with a jerk. In a great big hurry she half-carried, half-dragged him across the street. Then dumped him on the grass between the street and the sidewalk. Thank God no cars were coming.

By the time I got over there, he had gotten himself up, then tripped and fell on the edge of the sidewalk, skinning his hands. Arsha was already a ways up the alley-way and couldn't be bothered even looking back. He was bawling, I was pissed, and Arsha was off in another world.

I got over it though. I guess. And by midway up the alley we were all caught up and walking together.

"Mister, don't you have a wife?"

"No." I tried hard to be abrupt.

"Well, don't you have any kids?"

"No."

"Well, why don't you?"

"Well, why doesn't your mother have a husband?" I shouldn't have said it! I didn't mean to say it! It just came out. In sort of a bit of anger. Why the hell was she bugging me? Little bitch deserved it. But I shouldn't have said that to an eight-year old. I suffered for the next several minutes. And for a long time after that, really. Now what the hell if she tells her mother I said that? And an eight-year old will. The *bitch* will probably explode.

Arsha was quiet for a long time. I thought I'd better get her attention on to something else. I figured the ending of the school year was still a ways off, but maybe I could get her to talk about that.

"What grade are you in, Arsha?" My gut just went on wrenching as she didn't answer me for a long time. She just kept slowly walking along, brushing at the hedges that lined the right side of the alley.

"God, I was sorry I had said that. Damn, I wish she'd answer me. What the hell is she thinking?"

"Dack is my mother's husband."

I was stopped. I didn't know what to say. Dack! I had never realized that an eight-year old didn't know what a husband was. Or was it that she was just desperate for an answer. And that was the only one she could think of. Dack!

For just a moment I had a deep shudder that he might be Bibbie's father. But husband? I was sure the two weren't married. People like that just aren't married.

We just went on slowly. Didn't say anything.

Bibbie had toddled about all he was gonna. And Arsha sure wouldn't be carrying him any more that trip. So I had to pick him up and tote him the rest of the way, soaked and all.

Then out of the blue, "I'm in the third grade." She said it sort of quietly, then nothing else.

I guess I just said back to her, "Third grade," and didn't say anything else either. I was still fumbling with what to say to her about "Dack is my mother's husband."

We were still edging slowly up the alley when I see her friend coming at us – the one she had played jump rope with a couple of times on the front sidewalk. I never had gotten her name.

"Your mother is down there screamin' for you, Arsha. She's madder than I can say. Where have you and Bibbie been?"

Arsha hurried up ahead to meet her. They said a couple of things to each other I couldn't hear, then rushed off around the corner and down the block toward the building.

By the time I made it up to the end of the alley, I could hear the *bitch* still screaming at Arsha. Best I could see, though, she wasn't doing anything to her physically.

Well before I could limp down there with Bibbie, Arsha disappeared into the front door. Her mother then, just stood there on the sidewalk, glaring at Bibbie and me as we got closer. She did glance up at their apartment window a couple of times, thank God to break her glare. Closer we got, her eyes were directly on Bibbie, and not at me.

I mumbled out, "Sorry, ma'am, I thought they had permission." I didn't say it very well.

Without saying anything back to me, she grabbed Bibbie from me, and in a fit of rage, charged into the house and up the stairs.

I had just managed to sit down on the front stoop. I was tired as hell from all that. All of a sudden there was this sickening wail, and loud painful sobbing. A couple of things slammed – one may have been a door – and a dull thud. Their front window was open. It was always open. And I could hear it all.

"Jesus Christ, what is she doing? Has she hurt them? God, it wasn't my fault? God, I hope she hasn't hurt them bad!" I'm flustering.

Then up the sidewalk comes Dack, looking straight ahead, glazed eyes, no expression, as always. Unhappiest looking son-of-a-bitch you'd ever see. As always. Leaps up the steps, into the house, and up the stairs.

Then quiet. All's quiet. I can't hear a peep, for a long time. Then, finally, Dack's voice, not loud enough to hear clearly, snarling about something. Then, after a bit of that, quiet again.

I didn't sleep much that night. Maybe the stuffy odor, maybe the worry. I was down sitting on the stoop early next morning. Reading the neighborhood paper they drop by for free once a week. Never anything very interesting in it. But I read it once a week for something to do.

While sitting there, I'm thinking I gotta think of a way to get to the park without those two following. Although, after yesterday, that may not be a problem. "God, I hope they're both okay."

I began to hatch a plan where I would up my trips to the corner grocery from every other day to every day. Then I'd combine that with a trip to the park, at least on those days I wanted to go to the park. Those two had never seemed to want to tag along on my grocery trips. And I'd be headed the opposite direction we take to the park. That way I'd just go right on past the grocery, loop around the block to the park, and then come back the same way, picking up a few groceries on the return trip. If Arsha were to eventually catch on – and the little bitch might – then I'd have to come up with a different scheme.

"Why in the hell am I letting those two run my life like this? Damn! Wonder if they're okay?" While this was all going on in my head, the landlady, Mrs. Kline, pulls into a parking place a couple slots down. "That's twice in a week. She must be on the *bitch*'s case pretty heavy now."

We exchanged good morning, but instead of heading into the house to go after the *bitch* for her overdue rent, Mrs. Kline explains she'd like to talk to me about a matter.

"What's up?"

"Well, you know Charles, the young man who lives there in the first floor apartment?"

"I've seen him a couple times, but never met him." And don't want to, I thought to myself. Weird bastard.

"Well he's told me that he's moving at the end of the summer. And I thought considering how difficult it must be for you to climb the stairs to the third floor you might like to switch – move down to the first floor – after he's out?"

Sounded like a good idea. But I'd taken that third floor apartment because the rent was so low.

"I can keep the rent the same. I know you are on a steady income, with your disability, you know. And it is worth it to me not to have to go through a hassle every month just to get paid. And I already have a likely renter for your present apartment if you move down."

Sounded real good to me. Those stairs were sure as hell getting to be a pain. We struck a deal. I'd have to sign a new lease. She'd bring the papers by in a couple days, and I'd move at the end of the 30 days.

Then she looked me right in the eye and pointed up to the second floor apartment. "Do you know if they are up and about yet?"

I didn't. Hadn't heard a stir. So she left without bothering.

"Now that's gonna make life easier. Won't have quite the view from down here. And maybe a little more street noise. But saving all those damn steps. Man."

I pondered it all for a long time. Thought about what I'd do with all the time I'd save. And how I wouldn't have the shitty experience of passing the *bitch* or Dack on the stairs any more. Not that it happened all that often. But neither of them had ever as much as said hello – or even looked me in the eye.

Then I started wondering about the two brats. As it was now, they never, ever came up to the third floor. No reason to. And it might have been a little scary if they'd ever even thought about it. I'd never seen them bother that weirdo who's been living there. But then, to them, he's probably scary in his own right. "But what if they start pestering me?

Knocking on my door to do something for them? Or what if they make more noise than I expected?"

Well, anyway, thinking about all these nightmares didn't matter. I'd already agreed to move. And although I might'a backed out – landlady would be pissed – I figured I'd just go ahead with it. Hope for the best. Those two brats really were starting to control half my life. Son-of-a-bitch. "You know, I really need to find a friend or two. Somebody to talk to. This is drivin' me nuts. Nobody but those two brats, day in and day out. I gotta get over to the park and at least meet some people. By myself!"

Well, I'm just sitting there on the top step of the stoop, where I always sat, thinking about this. I heard the front door slowly open and as I turned half way, to see if I needed to get more out of the way, here comes Arsha, quietly lugging Bibbie out.

She didn't say anything, or look at me. She just kept struggling with him 'til they were down onto the sidewalk. He was just fussing lightly but not enough to give her a problem – other than that he was a load for her.

I hadn't had a very good angle on them, and once she put him down at the bottom of the stoop, she more or less kept her back to me. Just wandered down the sidewalk a few feet and began slowly walking through her hopscotch tracks.

But Bibbie soon turned toward me to grab hold of the porch rail post at the bottom step. And oh my God! His face – and his left arm! His left eye was swollen shut, all black and blue. His right cheek bone was cut and scraped. And he had other bruises on his face and all over his left arm.

My blood seethed. It's hard to describe what I'd like to have done to the *bitch* at that moment.

While I was boiling over that, I glanced down the sidewalk toward Arsha. She had turned toward me but was looking down at her feet as she slowly retraced her hopscotch tracks. Somethin' wasn't quite right. Then she looked up for a moment. There, for Chrissake, she had a large black and blue welt on her forehead! Nasty! Nasty-lookin' welt! She quickly looked back down and turned to slowly do her steps the other direction. Bibbie just played with a stick.

I was so shook up. I couldn't say anything to them. I didn't know if I should, or not. But I couldn't. It's probably a good thing that neither the *bitch* nor Dack came by at that time. I don't know what I'd have done. But it wouldn't have been good.

I rested my face onto my hands and anchored my elbows down on my legs just above the knees. I just sat there with my eyes closed for a long time. Arsha may have thought I was quietly crying. I probably looked like it. Anyway, while I just sat there wondering what to do, she quietly slipped up to Bibbie, picked him up and started toting him down the sidewalk. I figured she was probably trying to get away from me so she wouldn't have to answer any questions.

I felt so goddamn sorry for her. I surely felt terribly sorry for Bibbie, but I felt a special sorrow for her. If it weren't for her, who would Bibbie have?

I wondered how many other times this kind of thing had happened to them? Times I wouldn't have known about. Before I moved in. God pity this world. Why would people do that to little kids?

By the time she had struggled her way with Bibbie half way down to the corner, I decided it'd be better if I got out of the way. So I dragged myself up the stairs to the third floor and just sat in my apartment staring out the side window at the brick building next door. Seemed like hours.

Next day I didn't go out 'til late morning. I checked out my front window to make sure they weren't down there anywhere before going down. In fact, just as I did start down the top of the stairs I thought I heard their apartment door opening below, and I froze. When I was sure it wasn't opening I tiptoed as quietly as I could until I got outside, then headed down to buy some groceries. Luckily I made it back to my apartment without seeing either the kids or the two animals they had to live with.

Later I wondered why I hadn't used that day to sneak off to the park by myself. Just didn't have the stomach for it. Actually I spent the whole day in my apartment, blaming myself for not doing something about that terrible abuse. But I didn't know what to do.

It's amazing how quickly kids heal. By the second morning I was down on the stoop early as ever. Arsha and Bibbie showed up, as usual. Arsha's swelling was gone, and without looking closely you might have thought she'd just bumped herself lightly or something. Bibbie's eye was almost normal. And although he still had bruises on his arm, you might not have suspected anything unusual for a kid that age.

"Good morning," I said, gently as I could.

"Good morning," Arsha almost whispered, looking away at something across the street.

Slowly the rest of the morning carried on as usual. Arsha's friend showed up to play girl games. And Bibbie played with whatever he could find on the sidewalk around the stoop. And I just sat there and enjoyed the sunshine.

# CHAPTER NINE

## *Philadelphia - Early May*

Homer was relieved that Bull was not in the visiting team clubhouse as he sneaked in quietly to dress quickly and to get the devil out for pre-game warm-up.

About one hour before game time Bull had been served a subpoena from the City of Philadelphia for not having returned the phone message they contended they had left that morning at the hotel. Apparently they had wanted his agreement to start the game five minutes late that evening so the local TV coverage could broadcast the grand finale drawing of the Pennsylvania Lottery, uninterrupted.

Actually, the hotel had failed to communicate the message to Bull's room. But that was irrelevant. The Lawyers' general manager was upset and the TV station was upset, so they served the subpoena. Bull was enraged. The Flags' general management had initially been contacted, but they had asked that it be left in Bull's hands, which was why he'd supposedly been called. When he finally settled down, he agreed to the delay, but it was too late. He, or rather the Flags, had to pay the Philadelphia Lawyers a much negotiated $5 million to settle the matter.

During pre-game warm-up, Homer had noticed some bursts of booing from groups of fans in various parts of the stadium. He hadn't thought much about it. It hadn't seemed directed at anyone in particular. Jose explained it later, after the loud and persistent booing of every Flags' player's introduction just before the game. That had been followed by even louder and more vehement booing of every Lawyers' player taking the field.

Such fan support puzzled Homer until Jose described the long-standing Philadelphia tradition.

"Homer, didn't you notice that they even boo the bat boys and the ball girls? It's highly organized booing, you see. Did you notice those fans who stand up and face the crowd in the various sections? They're called the boo leaders. It's all taken very seriously here in Philadelphia, booing is."

Homer understood.

Just as the game was about to begin, and the first pitch was about to be thrown, somebody came running out of the Lawyers' dugout area and handed the home plate umpire a note.

The other umps quickly raised their hands for a time out. As the players on both teams backed off and relaxed – fooling with their gloves, and their caps, and their bats – the home plate ump appeared to re-read the note three or four times -- fooling with his cap and scratching his head. He then walked out into the infield and called the other umps into a conference.

After several more minutes of head scratching and fooling with their caps, the umps abruptly called the game and walked off into their locker room under the stadium.

The booing was deafening. Nobody could hear the PA system announcement. There was a sudden flurry of intense telephone activity in both dugouts. Then both teams were hurried into their respective clubhouses where the explanations could be heard.

Bull was quickly put under a sedative, and the announcement was left to Hank. The details, as he understood them, were: Apparently one of the umps had made a disparaging comment about the Philadelphia fans just before game time.

It had been overheard by a city official. Thus, a hastily prepared court order had been issued halting the game, if not the season. All would be in abeyance until the appropriate legal measures against the guilty ump had been decided upon.

That was all too complicated to try to convey to the fans over the PA system. They couldn't have heard it anyway, considering the decibel level of the booing. So very few of the fans, all of whom were handed rainchecks as they exited, understood what had happened until they heard it described on the evening news back in their respective homes and taverns.

The whole matter was settled the next morning after the umpires had threatened to strike. The city official had gotten unprecedented TV coverage the night before. So having achieved his goals, the court order was remanded, and the game of baseball survived another day.

Next evening, as the teams slowly filtered into their clubhouses, Hank managed to convince Bull that both he and Homer had suffered enough, and that Homer should be credited with a night off, even though the previous night's game had never been played. Bull grumped, but begrudgingly agreed to reinstate Homer as the DH, at least for this game. But it was a hollow victory.

First Flag up in the top of the first pounded a home run over the left field wall. The next three batters reached base, and there was a pitching change. Next man up, Homer Minley, the PA system announced to a raucous chorus of boos.

Homer fouled the first two pitches off and then took one high and inside nearly nipping his chin. In ducking the pitch, he had turned so that he was directly facing the umpire. Thus, when he cut loose with a sharp line of epithets, the ump mistakenly thought they were directed at him. Homer was immediately ejected from the game, followed by Bull. Bull's ejection was clearly deserved, but justice was not important to Bull right then.

The two of them showered and dressed at opposite ends of the clubhouse with not a word exchanged. This was certainly commendable on Bull's part. On Homer's, it was just fear. Bull retired to his private cubicle to watch the game on TV. Homer watched it on the big screen out in the players' area with the sound on mute.

The game was routine and boring to Homer (the Flags eventually won it 5 to 4). Homer had daydreamed his way through the three middle innings, wondering what Rover was up to and if he'd still remember Homer. He set his mind to go back and see old Rover, and his parents too, first time the team had a day off.

In the stands the game had not been at all boring. Early in the second inning a routine foul ball had landed on an empty seat way down past third base. It had frightened the devil out of some woman in the next seat. And although the ball had never actually touched her, she had sued for damages – emotional trauma, etc. A couple of months later a Philadelphia jury had awarded her $4.5 million for her extraordinarily severe experience.

By coincidence, another lawsuit filed by another fan at the same game had also been a costly one to the Lawyers' organization. It seems that a seven-year old fan had received life-threatening burns (they had all healed by the following evening) from an overheated hot dog his father had gotten him on their way into their section of the stands. Apparently the jury members had tears streaming down their faces as the plaintiff's lawyer had described the pain and agony the boy had suffered as a result of the crass and careless -- with a total lack of concern for their fans' safety and welfare – way the grossly irresponsible Philadelphia Lawyers' management had allowed (well, not just allowed, but egregiously aided and encouraged) the totally money-hungry and neglectful practices of the almost subhuman vendors under contract at that particular game. The jury ultimately awarded the boy's grieving parents $3 million for their life-scarring ordeal.

In addition to the ball club itself, several others were named as defendants in the suit: the contract vendor who'd sold the hot dog (filed for bankruptcy the following week); the young woman employee who'd callously handed such a scalding hot dog in a bun to the father and had collected the $4.00 for it (she fled town a few days later); the manufacturer of the hot dog cooker (settled out of court for an unnamed amount); the meat packing company who'd produced the hot dog (also settled out of court); the paper producer who'd supplied the hot dog wrapper; the mustard supplier (whose mustard had miraculously survived the blistering heat of the hot dog – along with the father's hand which had held the hot dog bun while applying the mustard); and several lesser defendants who pleaded no contest.

The appeals were all dismissed, the awards were paid, and ticket prices were duly increased.

Now these court proceedings and pain and suffering awards had all taken place long after the Flags had left town. But they weren't the only headline stories as a result of that three-game series – well, actually two.

In the final game of the series Homer had been walked five times and had scored three times. The Flags had won the game 12 to 7, but not without incident.

In the bottom of the fourth, the Lawyers' batter had hit a ball down the first base foul line. As the ball curved toward the stands, Tony Springfield, the Flags' right fielder, reached into the front row of fans to grab it for one out. But at the last moment the boo leader for that section – he felt a special responsibility – grabbed Tony's arm instead, causing Tony to drop the ball.

Tony exploded! He had whacked the boo leader twice over the head with his glove. By the time the boo leader had escaped back into the third row, the umpire and a security officer were on the scene. Tony settled down as quickly as he had blown up. He trotted back to his right field position, the ump returned to his, and the game resumed.

But the security officer, most sensibly, checked with the boo leader to be sure he was okay. Understanding the system, he wailed a little bit, complained bitterly of severe neck pain, but respectfully had to get back to his duties at hand.

The post-game result of all this was, of course, a multi-million dollar lawsuit against Tony and the Flags' organization. Oddly enough, both the umpire and the security officer testified on Tony's behalf. The case was then settled out of court for an undisclosed sum.

But in the meantime Tony had been charged under a 1799 Philadelphia city ordinance for ungentlemanly like conduct. His attorney was able to find a cooperative Philadelphia law firm, who for a small sum, was able to arrange for the charge to be dismissed.

The final results of the three game series:

Flags, won 2.

One game rescheduled at a later date.

Homer's batting average – still 1000.

Homer had thought that maybe his older brother, Joe, might show up for one of the games in Philadelphia, but he didn't. He thought Joe lived somewhere in the area, at least according to his dad. He had even tried to call Joe at the number his dad had given him: the phone had rung three or four times; then it sounded as though somebody had picked it up to answer it. Homer said, "Hi, Joe?" That was followed by a long silence. Then it just clicked, followed by a dial tone; and Homer, all confused, didn't try again.

## CHAPTER TEN

# *Wilmington – Early June*

Early May, Dad had called. Wanted me to go to a baseball game in Philly when Homer'd be there with the Flags. Too much hassle. Besides, I wouldn't go see the dumb bastard play anyway. Never could get over – Homer wouldn't even be around if Maggie hadn't drowned. Then Mom had to have another kid. But Homer could never replace Maggie. No way.

Early June Arsha's summer school began. The kids and me hadn't seen much of each other since the incident. I guess they hadn't been out front much. And I hadn't either.

It had been drizzly and overcast a couple days. Then I'd actually tried out my new scheme to slip off to the park by myself. The one sunny day it had worked. I'd gone by way of the grocery both ways. The little brats never knew what happened. I had felt a little guilty after what they'd been through. But I just needed to try it once, to see if it worked. I hadn't really talked to anybody at the park. But it'd been a great relaxing day.

That Sunday evening was pretty nice, and I was just enjoying it, sitting out there in my favorite spot. The kids had showed up, kind of quietly. Bibbie had quickly gotten into his play routine down on the edge of the sidewalk. He was giggling at something, as he sometimes did, for no reasons I could ever figure out. Dumb kid.

Arsha had been down that part of the sidewalk she usually played. But she had slowly worked her way up near the step where I was sitting.

"Mister, did you know tomorrow's the first day of summer school?" The way she said it I could tell she had something on her mind.

"Yeah, I heard you mention it last week."

There was a long pause. She finally looked up directly at me. She usually wasn't so shy, but she was having trouble saying something.

"I don't have no way to get there."

"Wha'da you mean?"

"Well, school starts at 7:30, and my mother is on night shift. And she won't be back in time to take me."

I don't know why I did it, but I did. If the *bitch* didn't care a damn bit about her kids, why should I? I guess it was because I felt so damned sorry for them – having to live like that.

Anyway, I was up and dressed by seven o'clock that Monday morning, waiting for Arsha down on the front steps. And holy crap, here she comes, dressed as pretty as she could manage, and with Bibbie! I don't know how I could have overlooked Bibbie. But what else was she to do with him? You'd thought I'd have been pissed. To have to get up that early to do something that wasn't any of my business. But when they came out the door, and she was all dressed up so pretty, I was near dumbfounded at how she'd gotten Bibbie all cleaned up and dressed.

"Have you had anything to eat?"

"I gave Bibbie some juice and a muffin. He didn't eat much though."

"But did *you* have anything?"

I couldn't figure a kid going to school without somethin' to eat.

"No, I didn't have time."

"Well, wouldja like to grab something at the grocery on the way by?"

"No," she said after a few steps, as though she had her mind on other things.

I was toting Bibbie, of course. I toted him the whole damn four blocks to the school. I couldn't ask her to carry him part of the way and let him mess up her nice dress. And I couldn't put him down to toddle part way. He'd be too slow, and we needed to move.

We began to see other kids with mothers and grandmas and older sisters as we turned left at the corner onto Chester Street. Arsha was trying to look very proper. She kept a couple of steps ahead of me on the right. Next street we turned right and traffic really picked up. Bunches of kids all dressed up headed for first day of school. I wasn't even feeling my normal way about brats. Mostly, they seemed like Arsha; just trying to look real proper.

I wondered if she was embarrassed at having me walk her. I didn't see any other men. I must have looked like her dad. Whoever he was.

Bibbie squirmed a little bit from time to time. But all in all he was pretty good. I even patted him on his butt a couple of times just to thank him.

Arsha hadn't said anything the whole four blocks. And I hadn't wanted to bother her in her thoughts about the first day of school. I did kind of wonder what she was thinking though. Near the school she hurried ahead of us, then just turned and waved to us, kind of shy like.

Then I heard her say, "Bye bye Bibbie," and quickly turned and lost herself in the crowd headed up the front steps into school.

Bibbie started to fuss when she left. Then he started to cry. Then he held out his chubby little arms her direction and cried harder. I had put him down for a moment just before Arsha was out of sight, and he had tried to toddle after her. But he had fallen forward, like he did a lot of times when he tried to hurry. He had caught himself with the palms of his hands flat on the sidewalk. So he didn't skin his knees. By that time she was out of sight. So he just bawled.

A couple of other brats were bawling and clinging to their mothers so as not to have to go into the school. Must have been first graders.

I tried to pick Bibbie up to head back. But he wouldn't have any part of it. Little bastard just kept bawling and fussing. I spotted a bench to sit on, so I figured I'd just wait him out. Didn't take long.

Shortly he was over wanting up on to my lap no less. I guess I was just getting too feeble to resist any more. Not that 28's that old. But well…whatever.

Anyway, he started fidgeting so damn much I finally put him down. Thank God he headed after a squirrel next to a tree nearby, then a cat over toward the school building, then a dog some woman was walking back toward the rear playground area. Lucky that was all in the school ground area, so I didn't have to go out and get him away from the street.

Bibbie finally settled down to playing with some sticks near by. And I'm just sitting there thinking about things in general, you know. All along I'd been wondering when the *bitch* was getting back to her apartment. And what she'd do when she saw Bibbie wasn't there. And what Arsha had told her about getting to school. And just how I'd get Bibbie back up to their apartment without having to deal with her face-to-face. I also wondered if she was going to walk Arsha back from school that afternoon.

"Well, Bib, better face up to it, and get our butts back home."

It took a while. Be damned if I was going to tote him the whole way back. So I'd carry him a ways, then let him toddle a ways; then I'd carry, then he'd toddle; and so on, until we finally got there to the front stoop where I collapsed onto my favorite sitting spot.

But Bibbie was restless the moment I put him down on the steps. I supposed it might be getting around time he'd be needing to potty. I couldn't tell if the *bitch* was back yet or not. But whether she was or wasn't be damned if I wanted to tote him up the stairs to that apartment and get all involved in that. I wished the little bastard would just sneak around to the side of the building and do whatever he had to do. I sure as hell wouldn't tell.

He was rattling away, as he usually did, in his jabbery baby babble, which I could never make head nor tale of. "Chot, chot, chot" or something like that. Maybe he was hungry. He'd look up at me, twist his face, and start whimpering. Then when I didn't do anything, he seemed to look for something to play with. Then after a minute or so he'd twist his face and whimper some more. Damn it! I wanted his mother to show up in the worst way. And I dreaded her showing up in the worst way.

Why the hell am I so up-tight about that *bitch*? She has never once said a word to me. Maybe a cold icy stare. But nothing more that I knew of. But damn!

I was just in the middle of getting ulcers over it when there she comes up the sidewalk, the other side of the street. I tried to ignore

Bibbie. And I sure as hell ignored her. I was wishing there was a newspaper or something I could be into as she approached.

Not a word. She simply whisked Bibbie up, charged into the building, and up the stairs. Last thing I heard was their apartment door close. Then quiet. And I could sit there peacefully for a while.

If I'd been a little lonely before that day, that was the loneliest day I'd spent since moving in. Not even the two brats to fuss about.

I finally got myself moving and made it over to the park. I even went the short way, down the alley-way. After all my figuring and scheming how to get to the park without having to fool with those two, here I am now with kind of an empty feeling. Damn.

I didn't stay long. The place was deserted. The playground area was empty, the ball fields were empty; even the bike path was empty.

The hot dog vendor must have not gotten the message yet, though. I'd seen him once before when the brats were with me. He was parked off around the bend in the bike track, hidden by the trees. I hadn't mentioned it then, hoping those two hadn't see him. They hadn't. Only reason I'd gotten a glimpse of him was the day I'd taken Bibbie back that side-path through the woods while Arsha'd been over on the swing sets. With her sharp eye she'd sure as hell have seen him if she'd been with us. The little bitch would have been after me nonstop to get them hot dogs, and everything else, if she'd seen him.

Anyway, today was different. I ambled over and got myself a dog with chili sauce with nobody pestering me. And that was my lunch. I said to the guy that he must not be selling many hot dogs today, with the kids all back in summer school. I could tell he didn't understand me. He jabbered something in another language. We just nodded to each other, and I left to find a bench for sitting.

"You know, goddamn it, I just can't win," I thought to myself. "I spend half my life trying to shed those two to get rid of all the pestering; now I kind of miss them."

I spent the next half-hour sitting there thinking about the brats. Should I go over toward the school around mid-afternoon just in case the *bitch* doesn't go to meet Arsha to walk her home? Why hadn't I checked with Arsha when I dropped her off? I didn't even know what time school let out. And it's a hell of a walk over there and back in my condition. Even without having to drag Bibbie along. I may have been feeling sorry for myself. Damn! I hated the thought of that. Or, maybe I was making excuses. Anyway, I put it out of my mind for a bit.

I started thinking about Bibbie. I sat there realizing that as much of a pain-in-the-ass he was I really felt sorry for the little guy. I wondered how much abuse he'd actually been taking in that rotten-hole apartment from the *bitch* and scum ball Dack. I'd hoped I hadn't just seen the tip of the iceberg.

And what would 'come of the little bastard with Arsha in school all the time now? Poor little fucker. Face it, I've gotten so I'm kinda attached to him. Son-of-a-bitch.

The thing about a little kid like that, he really doesn't have an evil bone in his body.

Ever since I'd known him the poor little devil had never had any little kid's toys to play with. At least none I'd ever seen. Nothing. Never even one of those little plastic things I used to see kids in my Philly neighborhood play with.

I remembered one of the first times I ever saw Bibbie. He'd grinned, sort of shy-like, and tried to hand me the little stick he was playing with. I kind of feel a little bad about it. 'Cause I was in a crappy mood that day. And I'd just ignored him. Then he just turned away and went on playing with that stick himself.

I'm sittin' there thinkin' about this and down the bike path comes a young mother wheeling a couple twins in one of those double strollers. They may have been a little younger than Bibbie, but not much. She was going a little slow so that they had time to look up at me as they came near. I guess I must have looked down at them and smiled. 'Cause they both gave me a great big smile – almost a giggle – and one of them wriggled his little legs and waved his arms like all joy was breaking out.

It made me think. You know, Bibbie never smiles all that much. Of course, what the hell does the little bastard have to smile about? When he does smile, he's cute as hell. But he just doesn't do it very much. Sometimes when Arsha picks him up, she'll talk baby talk to him and give him a little shake in a fun sort of way, and then she really gets him happy and giggling. But that's about the only time I ever see the kid really happy.

Sometimes I'd wondered what really goes on in that apartment up there. 'Specially when Dack is up there with the *bitch*. Christ knows what they are shootin' or smokin'. I hope they close the bedroom door. At least for Arsha's sake. In a way thank God she's there. She probably helps keep Bibbie out of the line of fire.

I hear Bibbie crying, and even screaming, from time to time. Can't help hearing with that front window open all the time. But I'd always figured that was just normal with little kids. They're gonna cry and scream some.

I swatted a large beetle that had just crept up onto the park bench. Probably wanted to taste my hot dog. You always want to sit on a bench that isn't too close to trees, at least this time of the year.

Then I'm thinking how funny it is, that when I first met those two, Arsha and Bibbie, how they'd constantly piss me off. And now I'm fussin' and frettin' about them as though I'm their dad or something. Maybe 'cause I never had any kids of my own. Maybe 'cause of how I think I see them treated. Whatever. I need somethin' to do with myself. I need to get off this crap. I'm getting' too soft. Fuckin' kids.

I'm about to get up and head back home – home; yeah – when I spot two, about 12-year olds, over under a big tree. One is lighting up his buddy. For Chrissakes. First of all, they oughta be in summer school. So here they are playing hooky first day over here smoking pot. Not that I had a big thing about pot. A lot of guys back in the shop smoked it. I didn't, but a lot did. But here's two 12-year-olds smoking pot. I shoulda reported the little bastards.

Instead of heading straight back, though, I had half a notion to go by way of the school. I was still worried about what if the *bitch* didn't bother to go walk Arsha home. What if she didn't have anybody to walk with? What if some creep offered her a ride home in his car? Those scum were always hanging around schools to target young girls. Or what if she got tangled up with a low class bunch like those two under the tree?

But then I thought, what if I go over there and the *bitch* does show up? And sees me? Then what? Goddamn it. I'd better go back and sit out on the stoop for a while first. See if she comes down out of her apartment and heads on toward the school.

I'd been sitting out in my spot for about 10 or 15 minutes and was starting to get a little edgy. Again, I didn't know what time school let out, but I hadn't seen the *bitch* at all. Then I thought I could see a couple school-age kids, with a woman, walk the opposite direction of the school.

I was looking down toward the corner grocery, and they were on the other side of Chester Street, hidden partly by the trees.

Then came another, with an older looking woman. Then came a whole bunch of kids. Damn it. I'm too late. School's already been out for at least five or ten minutes. And as slow as I am, it'll take me 20 minutes to get there.

So, about the time I'm bitchin' at myself about all this, around the corner by the grocery comes Arsha and two other kids, a boy and a girl. Soon as they got a little closer, I could tell, the girl was the same one Arsha had played with out front a few times. The boy? Never seen him before. Looked maybe a year or so older than Arsha. Scruffy looking kid. Dark, curly hair hangin' all over the place.

The three of them must have walked back here together without anybody meeting any of them. Must be okay if there is three of them. Or maybe I just don't understand.

About that moment, while the three of them are slowly headed up the sidewalk, I hear a shriek from the upstairs window. "Bibbie!" That's all I heard. No crying or screaming, or any more shrieks, just quiet then.

"Well at least they're up there. At least that."

The closer Arsha and the other two got, the more I could hear the scruffy kid using a bunch of foul language. I'm not any prissy mouth, but I don't foul mouth in front of kids, especially girls.

They didn't pay much attention to me, but I wanted to know what was up.

"Have a good first day?" I tried to get eye contact without luck.

Arsha finally answered; "It was fun," and then went right on chattering with her two friends. She finally stepped over to the stoop to put her backpack down.

"Whose your buddy?"

"Darren." She was fiddlin' with something in her backpack but still wouldn't look at me.

"He in your class?"

"No, he's my cousin." Then she went right back over to them and that was all I was gonna get out of her.

A couple of minutes later they split, and Arsha headed straight up to her apartment without saying boo to me.

And for the rest of that week, I barely even saw her. Didn't see Bibbie at all.

Her mother must have walked her to school each morning. I never did see them leave, but I'd see the *bitch* comin' back up the sidewalk on her return. We never even looked at each other, but that had to be where she'd been. I couldn't stand her guts, and maybe she couldn't stand mine.

But where the hell was Bibbie? I couldn't believe she'd go off and leave him all alone up in that apartment for a half hour or more. Later I realized that Dack had probably been up there all that time. Probably sleepin' it off. What a big fuckin' help he'd have been if Bibbie needed it.

I was beginning to worry about Bibbie. At least when he'd been out front with Arsha, back before school started, I could see he was either okay or not okay. But at least I'd see him there in one piece.

I'd go over to the park for an hour or two every day that week. All by myself. I was lonely. Once I met an old fart with a cane. Thought we might have something in common. But he spent the whole time bitchin' about everything from his medical problems to his relatives to whatever the hell else he could think of. I finally just got up from the bench and left.

What few joggers and walkers and bikers there were going by were all in big hurries. Otherwise the place was nearly empty. In fact, I never even saw the hot dog vendor again. He must have decided to close up shop, with so few people around now that school had started. Besides, he couldn't speak English anyway.

When you have spent your time workin' in a shop, with plenty of people to talk to, you don't realize how you're gonna miss that some day.

Didn't want to admit it to myself then, 'cause kids had always seemed like such a pain in the ass. I'd really begun to miss Arsha and Bibbie! At least I knew where Arsha was. But Bibbie?

## CHAPTER ELEVEN

# *Boston – Mid June*

Early morning, on the flight to Boston, Homer and Jose shared a copy of the *Baltimore Sun*. With the Flags now alone in first place, the Flags' players were all hometown heroes. Bull's biography consumed half a page in the sports section, and there was a photo of the old batting cage in Marietta where Homer had first demonstrated his skills. One of the local TV stations had sent a reporter to San Pedro to interview Jose's family. Other stations had featured the backgrounds of various other Flags' players in a series of human interest stories.

So all was well as the team arrived at Logan Airport that Friday morning. Bull even attempted a lighthearted comment as they boarded the charter bus for the ten-minute ride to the hotel. This was to be a three-game – Friday, Saturday, Sunday – series against the Socialists who had already slipped back into second place in their division.

In most seasons the Socialists would battle their way to first place right up until September, then collapse. This season they seem to have started their slide a few months early.

It had seemed like an awfully long ten-minute bus ride to Homer. He could hear Bull snoring for over an hour of that. And then at an hour and forty-five minutes, Bull had awakened and had roared: "What in the hell are we doing in Concord?" It seems that the bus driver was relatively new to the Boston area. To avoid several blocks of street reconstruction in the tunnel area, leading from the airport into the city, he had made a wrong turn.

Jose later explained to Homer that "wrong turn" was an oxymoron in Boston, since there was no such thing as a right turn (referring to correctness rather than direction). Homer didn't quite understand it all. But thank heavens Bull had found something other than Homer to shed his wrath on.

Several hours later, having toured Watertown, Brookline, and Lynn, the bus finally arrived at the hotel. Bull had been given a sedative and was snoring peacefully. Under League rules, the game had to be forfeited by the Flags due to "unavoidable delays in the arrival of the visiting team."

The pubs in the Boston area were heavily burdened that Friday evening. Homer and Jose stayed in their hotel room watching TV as the New York Capitalists played their annual mid-season exhibition game against their AAA farm team, the Montreal Separatists. Neither Homer nor Pedro understood why the handful of Montreal fans sang the "Marseillaise" rather than the Canadian National Anthem during pre-game.

At breakfast next morning Homer dutifully scanned the *Globe* sports pages. On the last page he found a display listing the Boston Socialists ticket information, including prices:

Male WASPS: $20.00
Other White Males: $15.00

Minorities: $10.00

Women: $5.00

Welfare Recipients: Free

Once at the ballpark it seemed like an awfully long time for pre-game warm-up and clubhouse waiting.

An announcement finally came through. The new umpire's car had been stuck in the tunnel area for seven hours trying to get in from Logan Airport with no break in sight. The game was delayed for one hour. Then, it was delayed for another hour. By the time it finally got underway, half the fans had left. The pubs did an even greater business that second evening.

Since Boston was in the All Wide World League, which still did not have the designated hitter rule, Homer was not in the lineup. His only opportunity would be as a pinch hitter. And that opportunity came in the top of the ninth inning.

The game had dragged on forever. By 11:00 p.m. the game was tied 8 to 8. Homer was about to chuck it and head back to the hotel. It was past his bedtime. But just as he was standing up to stretch, Bull had condescended and had him beckoned to the on-deck circle. Bull had run out of pinch hitters, and with a change of pitchers coming up in the bottom of the inning, he was left with no choice.

Homer promptly sent the ball over the left field fence for a solo homerun putting the Flags up 9 to 8. But the Socialists tied things up in their half of the ninth, sending the game into extra innings.

Despite the late hour, Homer decided to stick it out. Baltimore's tenuous hold on first place was at stake. In the top of the eleventh, Boston's beleaguered pitching staff walked four straight Flags batters, walking in the go ahead run. The Socialists were unable to rally in their half of the eleventh. So at the stroke of midnight Jose threw out the Socialists' runner for the third out and a 10 to 9 Flags victory.

Homer was tired. But he was still batting 1000. And the Flags were still tied for first place.

At the bottom of page seven, in the *Globe*'s sports section the following day, was an almost obscure little article describing a new law, recently passed by the city of Boston, levying a tax on all visiting sports teams. It was for the purpose of supporting some Irish citizens group. Homer didn't quite understand the gist of it all, but he hoped that Bull hadn't seen the article. Bull had seen it, but he had bigger problems to worry about – holding on to first place.

Homer had shared a cab to the ballpark with a couple of other Flags' players that afternoon. But as they approached the players' entrance, they were stopped from entering by a group of protesters dressed in some strange-looking garb and wearing banners with various vulgarities describing both the Boston Socialists and Baltimore Flags' organizations. In an adjacent cab, Homer could see that Bull was being restrained by a couple of the coaches. Some police officers were calmly discussing the affair with a group of the protesters. They finally whacked three of them over their heads with billy clubs and ushered the Flags into the stadium.

Once everybody was safely in the clubhouse, an explanation filtered around. Apparently it was a group of college students who had found nothing better to do for the summer, protesting the fact that neither team had any Native Americans on their rosters, and that the season should be suspended until that egregious abuse was corrected.

But all was soon forgotten. For no sooner had Homer and his teammates taken the field for pre-game than into the field streamed the strangest looking band of fans Homer had ever seen. It was another protest but for a different cause. After hundreds had flooded the field, with numerous of them shouting their spokesmanship status, a couple of the Socialists' front office representatives were able to decipher the core of the issue. It seems that although welfare recipients were given free passes into the games, they had been expected to pay for their own hot dogs, sodas, and other concessions. This was an unacceptable burden, according to the "Boston Society for the Propagation of Freedoms for All." The group had been organized by a prominent local law professor. They had organized this massive protest by coaxing all potential beneficiaries onto the field with promises of free skyboxes and unlimited access to the respective gourmet buffets.

Homer had never been in a skybox, but he suspected those protesters were up to no good.

Hank, and the other coaches, managed to confine Bull to the clubhouse until the field had been cleared and the manager's presence was required for lineups and other duties.

In contrast to the previous night's game, this one zipped right along. Either both starting pitchers were doing a whale of a job or the hitters weren't.

At the end of seven innings, Boston led 2 to 1. The first Flags batter slapped out a single. Then following a strike out, the next took first on a base-on-balls. Then Billy Clark fell victim to another strike-out. Two out with men on first and second. Next up, Obie Long, Baltimore's starting pitcher. Obie was sporting a 106 batting average, and he was clearly beginning to tire on the mound by the late seventh inning.

In a rare state of frustration, Bull had asked Hank to make the call. "Homer, you're in." So as Billy Clark took his third strike, Homer calmly stepped toward the batter's box.

Fortunately for Baltimore, the Socialists' giant reliever was as arrogant as he was big. Homer took the first pitch, a 98 mph fast ball, right down the middle for a strike. He fouled the next two pitches off. Then a 96 mph fast ball just missed the outside corner. Count, one and two.

Next pitch was Homer's all the way. Another 98 mph fast ball right down the pipe, and right out into the right field wall, bouncing all over the place. Both runners scored easily as the right fielder chased the ball around in frustration. Homer even made it all the way to second base.

With the Flags now leading 3 to 2, the top of the order, Poley Lancaster, stepped in. Homer led off second one step; then two steps; then, beyond Bull's wildest imagination, three –

As Homer was easily picked off for the third out, Bull exploded onto the field, with a bat waving, headed straight for Homer. Hank, coaching at third, was the first to perceive the risk. He knew better than to try to stop Bull head-on. But as a former linebacker, he was mildly adept at tackling.

Now in his younger, speedier days, the 260-pound Bull might have posed a terror for the best of linebackers. But this night, as he lumbered by, Hank was able to drive a gentle tackle into his left side throwing him just enough off course to completely miss the petrified Homer who was frozen between second and third base.

To his credit, Boston's first baseman, who was about the size of Bull, managed to hustle over and grab the bat as Bull wobbled to maintain his balance. By then a number of players from both sides had gotten themselves between Bull and Homer to prevent any damage.

Jose had gotten hold of Homer and had ushered him quickly back through the dugout and right past the clubhouse door to one of the taxis queued up near the players' exit.

Bull was, of course, ejected from the game and fined $20,000 by the Commissioner of Baseball for conduct unbecoming a manager.

Most of the fans considered it all the most entertaining ten minutes since the Flags had arrived in Boston. The scene was run and rerun several times on the 11:00 p.m. news that night in Baltimore.

The 3 to 2 score had held, and Baltimore had gone on to win the game and stay in a tie for first place.

The Flags' management had quickly drafted an apology statement for Bull. At next day's press conference it was read on his behalf by a Flags' spokesman.

For the sake of prudence, Bull did not return to Baltimore with the team, but was put onto a commercial flight arriving at BWI an hour later than the others.

The incident was the buzz in every coffee shop in Baltimore the next morning. But then too were the Flags' two victories and one forfeit in Boston. And so was their continuing hold on their first place position in the division standings.

And as things progressed, by late June, the Baltimore Flags win-loss record was a phenomenal 44 and 16. And Homer was still batting 1000.

## CHAPTER TWELVE

# *Wilmington – Late June*

First I could hear some screamin' and some bumpin' and some thuds. Not all that unusual from that apartment. But this time their door was open. I had just started up the steps.

I'd been sitting out on the stoop and was headed in to fix a coffee, when, in all the racket, Arsha comes running down the stairs past me. What the hell she doin' home in the middle of the day, I wondered.

Things got worse. Dack was barkin' a flood of obscenities and other sounds I couldn't understand, and the *bitch* was screaming somethin' back at him. And they got louder. By the time I made it up to their landing, things were getting real bad.

I'd never really seen inside that apartment before, and I shouldn't of this time. But Arsha had left the door wide open in her rush out. And at the pace I could move was no way I could avoid seeing right in. It was horrible. It looked like Dack had thrown the *bitch* down back in a corner next to an old beat-up sofa. But worst of all, Bibbie was screaming and crawling down off the sofa and Dack just bolted at him and grabbed him and threw him toward what I guessed was a bedroom door. Just threw him! I couldn't tell if he missed the door or what, but my stomach turned as I heard him thud against something. Then a moan and gasping and quiet… Oh God, in that seconds of quiet it was horrible. Then some more gasping. Dack was half snarling, half bellowing, “Get that little fucker out of here!” at the *bitch*.

I didn’t know what the hell to do. It was horrible. In my state I couldn’t have taken Dack on, but I had to do something. The *bitch* was moaning and sobbing and garbling out some kind of threats at her rotten scum boyfriend. He just laughed at her in a disgusting babble of jargon I couldn’t make head nor tail of.

Bibbie had switched from gasping to an awfully uneven sobbing. I just prayed he had no head or neck injuries, or anything like that.

All of a sudden Dack just sits down in a dilapidated old easy chair – its stuffing comin’ out through the ripped cover – and just stares straight ahead in a glazed stare. Just no movement. Just straight ahead into a corner of the room. He just sat there.

The *bitch* finally struggles up, moaning and bitching a stream of vulgarities, and stumbles over to where Bibbie had landed. I didn’t think she or Dack either one had seen me yet. Least I didn’t think so. I was just standing there, dyin’.

I was feeling such a mix of rotten guilt for not doing something earlier; for not trying to help. God, what if my fear of getting involved had cost that little bastard’s life? No, it couldn’t have been that bad. But what if he was badly injured? Oh, what a miserable asshole, I am, I suffered to myself.

I finally looked in at the *bitch* as she was huddled down on her knees, checking Bibbie over; “Can I help with anything?” I half whispered. She just looked at me kind of blank-like; then back at Bibbie. She never answered.

The nightmare had been on Thursday. After not much sleep that night, Friday dragged on slowly and miserably. I saw nobody until Arsha came walking home by herself from school.

"How's Bibbie doing?" I just blurted out at her as soon as she got close. It was sort of a dumb way to greet her, just point blank like that.

"Okay," she said quietly, not even looking at me. She went right on up stairs.

I sat out there a little longer, then went on up to my apartment.

Saturday went a little better. Actually, Arsha brought Bibbie down front around mid-morning. He seemed okay. At least I couldn't tell if anything was wrong. He may have had some light bruises in his rib area when his little t-shirt pulled up as she was putting him down. But nothing more than that. Even so, I was beginning to wonder more seriously if I shouldn't notify some child abuse agency about things I'd seen and suspected since I'd been living there. "Maybe Mrs. Kline'll be by one of these days and I'll ask her who I should call."

Anyway, Bibbie gave me a little smile when Arsha sat him down. Then he went chasing a big spider running along the side of the steps down on the sidewalk.

Arsha was even a little talkative. We talked about how her school was going. She liked her teacher and was all happy about her art class. Her friend, whose name I had finally figured out was Bandi, came by after a bit, and they jabbered about school and classmates and some boys they didn't like.

I began thinking, you know, they're pretty decent kids. I was feelin' kind of upbeat. And Bibbie was as bubbly as I'd seen him in a while, down there giggling about some new bug he'd gotten after. What the hell. Why don't I ask if they'd like to go to the park?

"I'll even buy you all a hot dog." I'd forgotten the hot dog man hadn't been there last time.

"Can Bandi come too?"

"Sure. But you two have to help carry Bibbie part way."

Bibbie had to stop five times to explore everything from an ant hill to a chipmunk cutting across our path. The girls ran ahead to the playground area and the swing sets. They ran into a half dozen other kids from their school and were soon having a ball – laughing and swinging and chasing each other around.

Bibbie and I had a ball too. I took him on the teeter totter and the little merry-go-round thing and the jungle gym, and then he wanted to do it all again. Little bastard wore me out. But I was enjoying it. First time I'd enjoyed anything in months.

And we had a few laughs that day, Bibbie and me. He'd start giggling about something, and it would catch my funny bone, and I'd chuckle. And then he'd see me chuckling and he'd giggle even more. Just from the expression on his face there once or twice I suspected he was surprised to see me chuckle. Then he'd wave and wriggle his chubby little arms all in excitement and delight.

I'd never seen him brighten up his big brown eyes like he did that day. They'd always been sort of dull looking in the past. Even half afraid like. But he really opened up that day at the playground. And so did I. I was almost jealous when the girls came over and wanted to take him on the teeter totter again. Their friends had had to leave and go home, and Arsha was ready for a new scene anyway. So they teetered Bibbie for a while, then got tired of that too, and went on to walk the bike path, up the direction Bibbie and me had been before.

Shortly, while I was trying to show Bibbie how to draw pictures in the dirt with a stick, they came running back all enthused about something.

"You know, Mister, you promised to buy us a hot dog?" all excited and out of breath.

"Yeah. I guess I did."

"Well, could Bandi and me have an ice cream instead?" she paused, and I paused.

"The ice cream man is right up around there." She pointed up around the bend in the path.

"And you and Bibbie could have one too." That was sure as hell good of her.

We all had different kinds of ice cream. The girls took theirs off to a bench by themselves, while I took Bibbie over to the nearest bench.

I'd gotten Bibbie a creamsickle, which I thought would be easier for him to eat. Be damned if I was gonna share my waffle cone with him. What a mistake. What a mess. Christ, he got it all over himself and all over me and all over the park bench. The goddamn insects had a field day.

Then he wanted a bite of my waffle cone after all. But he was so friggin' cute, the way he looked up all bug eyed, with a little grin, I couldn't get mad at him. So I gave him a bite.

Lucky, the ice cream man, saw what a sticky mess we were and walked over and handed me a damp towel to clean off with.

Then Bibbie had to pee. At first I wasn't sure what he wanted. It took me too long to figure it out. He did kind of a little pant and looked slightly guilty. Then, he looked up at me, first with a sheepish grin, but he quickly switched to a look of terror.

I'm sittin' there watchin' it soak through the front of his grubby little shorts and down both legs. For the moment I was half-pissed. But as I looked at the terror in his eyes, I wondered how many times in the past he'd been beaten and battered for just pissing his pants. After all, a little kid has to do it. I shuddered.

The towel we'd used to wipe the ice cream up was too sticky now to use for this. So I took it back to the guy and asked if I could bum a wad of paper napkins to dry Bibbie off as best I could. He laughed and handed me a batch.

"Arsha, you and Bandi put those ice cream wrappers in the trash can," I yelled over at them. I wanted to make sure we didn't leave any litter which could look bad on the guy.

A couple minutes later Arsha came running over all excited about something – Bandi following.

"Mister, Mister, did you know there's a carnival next week over on the other side of the park?"

"No, I didn't," I answered her, trying not to show any interest.

"Mister, we heard those people over there talking about it!" She pointed to a couple women with three young teenagers over near where they'd been sitting. "They said there'll be a merry-go-round and a Ferris wheel and all kinds of neat things!"

I didn't look straight at her. I kinda had mixed feelings. Somehow, kind of deep down, it sounded a little interesting. I mean I sort of wanted to check it out to tell the truth. May sound silly for a guy my age to want to go to a carnival. Though what the hell. I couldn't remember going to a carnival since I was a kid, I guess.

"Mister, could you bring us to the carnival?" she pleaded. "If I ask my mother if it's okay?"

I didn't answer her right away.

"Huh? Huh?" she pestered.

I was torn. I halfway wanted to go to at least take a look at it. But I didn't want to have to drag a bunch of damned kids with me.

I shouldn't have said, "Well, maybe; we'll see." That was the dumbest damned answer I could have given. But I didn't have the heart to just give her a blunt "no."

A few evenings later, after we'd all had our naps, there I came, dragging back over to the carnival: Arsha, Bibbie, and Bandi; all three, all cleaned up and dressed in fresh clothes. Son-of-a-bitch.

## CHAPTER THIRTEEN

# *Baltimore – Late June*

The Flags were happy to be settling in to a nine-game home stand hosting Los Angeles, Cleveland, and New York respectively.

Baltimore won all three games over the LA Smogs. Homer breezed through the first two games batting four for four and was hit once by a pitched ball. He also collected five intentional walks and a record 47 foul balls.

But the evening following that second game Jose and a couple other Flags' buddies had coaxed Homer into going out to some bars to look for girls. They found some. At the first stop, Homer, not understanding how these things worked, let slip to one of the girls that he and his buddies all played for the Flags. She kind of thought she recognized him from TV pictures anyway. Oh my goodness, the girls – all shapes and sizes and descriptions. They hovered, and they just kept coming. They called their friends on their cell phones, and more arrived. By midnight Homer was feeling a bit overwhelmed.

Jose had been through these scenes before. He had a plan. Pass the word around quietly, inviting selected ones to a party back at one of the player's apartment. Use a fake address, far from any actual address. Tell each one not to bring any friends. Homer was puzzled. He thought the whole idea was to find some girls.

"Yes, but not this band of losers," explained Jose. Then, Jose, followed by the other three, all amazingly, had to go to the men's room at the same time. Quickly by-passing it, they slipped out the back door, made a beeline for the car, and sped off down two back alleys and across town to an upscale after hours spot. And there they met some more – and well, more appealing girls.

After an hour or so there, just sipping and chatting, the four Flags with four friends, retired to Jose's spacious apartment for an actual party.

Homer slept late that next afternoon, as did his three buddies. And although they all showed up at different times, they all showed up late for the game that evening. One can imagine Bull's gentility as they each quietly slipped into the dugout during the first and second innings. Actually, Bull did manage to contain himself until the game was over, although a close observer might have noted a slight tightness and quivering of the jaw from time-to-time.

The Flags managed to eke out a 4 to 3 victory over the Smogs that evening, even without the assistance of Homer and his three buddies.

The clubhouse was an eerie quiet immediately following the game. The rest of the team quickly showered, dressed, and exited. Strange though, things remained eerily quiet. The team physician, always the prescient, had begun slipping small doses of sedatives to Bull as early as the eighth inning – this despite the closeness of the game. So that by the time the clubhouse explosion would normally have struck, nothing exploded. In fact, Bull dozed off.

Next day each of the four culprits was fined $5,000 and suspended for one game. And the media had a field day.

Following the three-game sweep of the Smogs, the Cleveland Mistakes arrived for only a two-game series at Ripken Field. Somehow the Flags struggled to a 6 to 5 victory in the first game in the absence of the four culprits.

Clouds had been forming in the skies over Baltimore late that afternoon prior to the second Cleveland game. By game time some thunder was rumbling off in the distance.

All four violators were back in the line up. But it was with sheepish anticipation as to the fans' reactions come pre-game introductions. But the crowd roared even a pinch louder for the long-absent heroes as each was introduced.

The rain started, just as Homer had drawn an intentional walk in the bottom of the second. After a 15-minute delay, it had tapered off enough to finish the inning. But before the first Mistake got to bat in the top of the third, a steady downpour had forced another delay.

And it rained; and for almost an hour it rained.

Homer fiddled and diddled – and exchanged a few brief inanities with some teammates. Then he crawled off into his corner of the dugout just to think. He thought about the antics that had gotten him into trouble two nights earlier. And he wondered why Bull was always mad. And he thought about New Somerton and his old high school sweetheart. And he wondered what his old buddies were up to now. And he wondered what Rover was up to now. He missed old Rover. He hoped old Rover missed him.

The rain finally ended, the tarp came off the field, and the game resumed. Top of the fourth, no score. The game remained scoreless when Homer was intentionally walked, again, in the bottom of the fifth. Then Broadway Bill slapped a line drive just clearing the left field wall and the Flags led 2 to 0.

The Mistakes came right back with two runs in the top of the sixth. Then in the bottom of the seventh, with the score tied 2 all, Cleveland's pitching got into trouble. They loaded the bases with nobody out and Homer coming to bat. What a hell of a predicament.

Do you give him an intentional base-on-balls, walking in the potential winning run? Or do you take the risk of pitching to this hitting terror? There was a long discussion on the mound. They discussed the options. First of all, there was no way to decide what kind of pitch to throw this teenage bumpkin. He hits everything thrown at him – didn't seem to matter: fast ball, change-up, curve ball, slider, whatever – Homer hit it.

Secondly, it didn't matter who threw it: leftie, right hander, side arm, whomever – Homer hit them. And there was no way to predict where Homer would be apt to hit whatever pitch they threw him. Even Homer didn't know that. But to intentionally walk in the winning run? What a mess.

The Mistakes made the wrong decision. They nipped the outside corner with a low slider. The crowd roared as the ball bounced off the right field wall, sending in three runs. Baltimore 5, Cleveland 2. And that score held as the final Cleveland batter grounded out in the ninth inning.

The Flags had taken all five games so far in this home stand, three from the LA Smogs and two from the Cleveland Mistakes. And the city and its fans were buzzing.

Attendance at Ripken Field was now up by 400% as compared to the average of the past five seasons. Bull had become a local celebrity, unusually articulate at charity functions and civic group meetings, and Homer had become a regular on TV sports interviews (with the interviewer doing most of the articulation).

The *Baltimore Sun* had begun running a short weekly column entitled "Homer's Hideaway." It was prepared by a ghost writer who described the intricacies of batting strategy and the ergonomic mechanics of effective hitting. Homer found the article interesting, although he didn't understand very much of it.

The next four games on the home schedule were to be with the dreaded and despised, New York Capitalists. Baltimore fans had always had a thing about the Capitalists; especially now, with the Flags and Capitalists tied for first place in the division.

In the first game, Baltimore won 6 to 5. Homer was on base five times: twice he was hit by pitched balls (intentionally), and three times on intentional walks.

Baltimore was now alone in first place, the fans were ecstatic, and every game in the series was a complete sellout. "Destroy the Capitalists," read the banner hanging from the skybox of Angelo Peters, owner and president of the Baltimore Flags.

New York panicked in the second game. They tried to pitch to Homer. In his first three times at bat he punched out three singles, driving in four runs. Baltimore led 4 to 3 as Homer stepped to the plate in the bottom of the eighth. With two out and with men on first and second, Hank hoped desperately that Homer would hit to right field – if they were dumb enough to pitch to him. They did pitch to him, but instead of right field, which should have allowed at least one runner to score, he drove a ground ball to left. It bounced into the left fielder's glove; he made an easy throw home to hold the runner at third. The next Flag batter flied out to center field and the inning ended (bases loaded) with the score still 4 to 3.

Bull had had it!

As Homer lumbered back to the dugout from his stranding at first base, he could see Bull's piercing glare – right at him – Bull's hands on hips, leaning slightly forward, ready to annihilate. Homer tried to divert slightly by looping the outside of third base en route to the dugout. It didn't work. Bull had maintained his ready-to-kill crouch while keeping himself on a beeline directly between Homer and Homer's dugout corner destination.

Homer prayed that he'd be accidentally hit and kayoed by a stray ball as the infield went through their round-the rosey warm-ups for the ninth inning. He considered running hard and jumping into the stands for safety, but then he thought better of it.

Bull didn't lay a hand on him. He just yelled. And he yelled. And he screamed. He screamed profanities Homer had never heard before. My goodness, did Bull lose his cool.

Hank tried discretely to intervene. But it didn't work. Homer tried to unobtrusively head into the corridor to the clubhouse. Bull followed, still screaming.

The only thing that saved Homer that evening was that the Capitalists went down in order on only four pitches in the top of the ninth, giving the Flags the 4 to 3 victory. The coaches, and some of the players closest to the door, went scurrying quickly into the clubhouse and were able to create a small crowd between Bull and Homer to reduce the attack to a low rumble.

Once someone had apprised Bull of the Flags' victory, he went grumping back to his clubhouse area, still blurting out death threats if "I ever got my hands on that imbecile."

Homer's name was not in the lineup the following day. And in spite of a brilliant pitching performance by the big left hander, Julio Juaguin, the Flags lost 1 to 0. In the press interviews following the game one of the obnoxious sports reporters asked the impertinent question, "Why didn't you play Homer tonight?"

"He's on a dumb-out," was Bull's response. Headline on the front of the *Sun's* sports page the following morning read, "Homer's dumb-out – or was it Bull's?" All Bull could do was to tear his copy of the sports page into a thousand pieces and swear never to answer a question from that reporter, ever again.

The fourth game against the Capitalists was rained out. So the Flags' final tally in the series was two wins, one loss, and a rain out.

During the Capitalists visit to Baltimore, in spite of Angelo Peter's unsportsmanship banner, "Detroy the Capitalists!," Joe Brineburner (principal owner and president of the Capitalists) was willing to deal.

All he wanted was to strike a side deal with the Flags. Joe demanded that since the Capitalists attracted such huge crowds at the games in Baltimore, there should be a 50/50 split in all revenues: ticket sales, TV and radio, and concessions. Peters was incensed. Brineburner agreed to only a 51/49 split, in total contradiction of the standard major league rules.

However, it was not a bad deal for Angelo Peters. Out of the agreement he got a waiver on the sealed bid process on some particularly valuable properties in Manhattan.

Meanwhile Homer had finally relented to be represented by "one of those sleezy agents" as his dad described them, and he was now beginning to garner some lucrative advertising deals. Although never allowed to speak, Homer's mug was seen driving an old jalopy in a TV ad run by Baltimore's largest used car dealer. And he was seen shopping for "valuable works of art (reprints)" in a newspaper ad by a local super discount store. He was even featured in an ad for "Gargle –Whiff" "after a tough night out on the town."

This was all to be very lucrative to Homer, as his agent agreed to compensate him 10% of net revenues earned from all the ads he appeared in.

But in spite of his financial success, a very disconcerting rumor had begun circulating. Word was that Bull was demanding that Baltimore Flags' management give Homer an unconditional release. "Get rid of him!" insisted Bull.

Of course, the moment the media got hold of the story, it became a veritable "Bull roast." They were relentless. And the fans responded. They poured into the games. All future games became sellouts. And they glued themselves to their TV sets to watch the biggest uproar in Baltimore since a retired governor had been caught running a major drug ring for nearby Washington politicians.

The problem it eventually presented to Flags' management was that both Homer and Bull became indispensable. Losing either could break the goldmine of revenues this conflict was generating.

Flags' management began daily press briefings to report on the Bull-Homer "situation."

Fans organized squads to "boo the Bull" and to "roar for Homer" at the games. They sent representatives to Philadelphia to learn more sophisticated booing practices. TV advertising rates skyrocketed in Baltimore.

And the revenues kept pouring in. The *Wall Street Journal* declared Homer and Bull the "most valuable pair in baseball."

## CHAPTER FOURTEEN

# *Wilmington – Early July*

"Arsha! You two stay close by here now. Don't go chasing all over where I can't see you!" I tried putting Bibbie up on my shoulders. He was totally lost down at ground level. It took me a bit to get him to hold on 'round my forehead. Then he nearly gouged my eyes out. But once he got his bearings, God was he excited.

The sun had just gone down, and people were pouring in droves. You could hear the music from the merry-go-round off the other side of some tents. All the noise from the rides and all those people was even a little exciting to me. Could imagine what it must have seemed like to Bibbie. Vendors shouting out cotton candy, and candied apples, and bratwurst, and all sorts of things. Arsha and Bandi had to have a cotton candy. Bibbie started hollerin', "Wa, wa, wa…" I let Arsha give him one try at it. He got it all over his face and his hands and my ears.

As it turned out Arsha had no money at all, and I reckoned later Bandi must'a had no more than a couple dollars. Damn it. I hadn't expected this. But once we were there I wasn't about to spoil things for those excited kids. So I anted up. Every time I turned around I was anteing up for something. Rides, hot dogs, games – for Chrissakes I must have spent $50 on them. Damn it. It was my own fault. But they had a ball.

Bibbie got so excited when he saw the clown I was afraid he'd piss his pants right up on my shoulders. He didn't. But I got his little butt over to the porta toilets first chance anyway.

The clown had come right over to us and had teased Bibbie with some of his antics. Wish I could have seen Bibbie's face. It must have been something else. He was giggling and shrieking and kicking his little legs and waving his little arms until I was afraid he'd fall off.

"Arsha! Get back over here. You're wanderin' too far away!" Had to constantly keep after them.

They'd spotted some ring toss game and wouldn't budge. So Bibbie and me went over to them. Some guy had just won a little teddy bear, and the girls were bug eyed. They wanted a teddy bear in the worst way, so I caved in.

"Go ahead, each of you gets three rings to throw."

They didn't even come close. Somehow, way back, I could remember those early disappointments as a kid. Funny how you can remember things way back like that.

"Mister!" Somehow Arsha's excitement had come back. "Mister! Could you throw the ring toss and get us a teddy bear?" She was bubbling.

And while this was all going on, Bibbie let me know that he'd like a teddy bear too. At least that's what I figured all his jiggling commotion was all about.

"Mister, please? Won't you please? Please?"

"Look, I'll try. Once. But don't get your hopes up." I was firm as hell. I needed to cut the garbage ahead of time in case I didn't win any prize. I missed all three tosses.

"Could you try again, Mis…?"

"That's it." I cut her off before she could finish her feeble whine. I quickly headed off toward the rides with Bibbie hanging on for dear life. He had gotten that crappy stickum from the cotton candy all over my forehead. Little bastard.

Soon as we got close to the merry-go-round, I put him down. Had to hold him right up close so he wouldn't get run over. It was getting crowded as hell, and now I'd lost track of the girls. Damn! I thought they'd followed me.

Finally, they came picking their way through. Once I'd gotten them all organized, I headed us over toward the merry-go-round. Arsha actually helped carry Bibbie 'til we got to the end of the ticket line. It was a hell of a long line. I'd seen that from aways back and figured that if I could get them interested, we could chew up a lot of time just waiting in that line.

It worked. Not that I wanted to stand in a long goddamn line. I was getting tired. But it beat the hell out of letting those two drag me all over the place spending money on them every two minutes. We were two turns back once we got our tickets. It took over 20 minutes and a bunch of whining. Bibbie was babbling "Wa…," again half the time. He only had two words, "Ba" and "Wa," and for the life of me I could never understand what the hell he was trying to say.

Somehow Arsha knew what he was talking about a lot of the time. She knew one "wa" from another "wa" and would explain to me what he was getting at when she thought I needed to know.

It was a relief to finally get on the merry-go-round. The girls scrambled for their pick of the horses. I put Bibbie on the first one I could get to and held him with my right hand while holding on to the post with my left. I wished someone else could hold him so I could sit down on one of those benches they had for adults.

Actually, it was kind of fun though. It brought back happy memories. That same old organ grinder music they'd played when I was a kid. I loved it. As it started up, the girls squealed and went into their goddamn sillies. And Bibbie? Well, Bibbie thought he'd just gone to heaven. I can't describe how Bibbie took it other than that he was one thrilled little fucker. Never seen him so happy. He was waving and giggling and kicking to a fare thee well. And he kept right on going while I was picking him up off the horse when it ended.

We weren't even off the platform yet when, "Can we go again, Mister? Can we go again?" I pretended not to hear her with all the noise and commotion. "Can we go again…?"

"Not right now." I was firm as hell. I headed over for a less crowded area near some big trees. Needed to get my bearings. The girls slowly tagged along. 'Well, could we ride the Ferris wheel, Mister?" She asked sort of quiet and hoping like. I didn't answer her for a while. She knew I'd heard her, so she didn't press her luck.

I stood there looking out over all those people having a good time; all the excitement and the rides and the music and the food tents and the like. And I thought to myself, "You know, I don't know if it'd be more fun if I could just come here by myself, not having to screw around with three brats; or is it more fun with them?"

Then I thought, "You know, three years ago you couldn't have dragged me to a goddamn carnival. Now I'm thinking like a 28-year old kid."

I gave in. We rode the Ferris wheel. I wouldn't have gone on it myself, except someone had to hold on to Bibbie. It stopped once when we were near the top and the girls screamed and shrieked and then froze. It scared Bibbie I think. He wasn't bubblin' like he had been on the merry-go-round.

By the time we'd gotten off onto solid ground, he looked like he was getting a little tired. I picked him up and he yawned. I took a look at Arsha and figuring I may have caught her in a weak moment, I told her we'd better head home before Bibbie fell asleep.

She whined a bit, and rattled off a list of all the things we hadn't done yet; all the time I was edging slowly toward the exit. She gave a feeble attempt to talk Bibbie into perking up. It was all he could do to keep his big brown bug-eyed fix on all the action slowly fading to our rear. So in spite of the pestering, I just kept slowly going, and after a few minutes, Arsha ran out of steam.

For the most part, it was a quiet walk home. It was pitch dark. I had to tote Bibbie all the way. When we got to the front stoop, I asked the girls if they'd had a good time. I was afraid I'd stomped on their fun, draggin' them away too early. But they both burst out with a whole bunch of "yea's!" and other happy jabbers. First time I'd heard Bandi say a word all evening.

About that time a couple women got out of a car parked a few spaces down from our stoop. They'd been parked there, for God knows how long, to pick up Bandi.

They were very polite. They made sure Bandi thanked me, then they thanked me quickly, and took off. I figured that Arsha had had to work all this out ahead of time. Not that it was all that complicated, but Arsha, I decided, was an organizer; maybe even a schemer. But in a lot of ways, she was a pretty sharp little kid.

Bibbie had slept on my shoulder the last half of the walk home. I handed him to Arsha and we all struggled up the stairs to bed. I paused for a moment on the stairs just above their apartment door hoping there wouldn't be any screaming and yelling when they went in. It was all quiet for several minutes so I went on up and quietly closed my door.

## CHAPTER FIFTEEN

# *Washington – Early July*

Pork Barrel Stadium, Washington, DC, home of the Washington Bureaucrats. From Baltimore it was only a thirty-minute drive so the players were on their own to get themselves to the ballpark. Homer would have had trouble finding it so he rode with Jose.

As they entered the visiting team clubhouse, they were quickly separated and each was escorted into a private cubicle. Each was handed a 63-page form, which all visiting players had to fill out to be eligible to play in Washington. Jose completed his in an hour and forty minutes. Homer took considerably longer.

Enough of the Flags had completed the task that Bull was able to present a lineup by game time. He was sweating that most of the intended starters would at least make it to the dugout by the time they'd be taking the field for the bottom of the first inning. But as it turned out his angst was for naught.

Great ceremony had been prepared for the local Congresswoman to throw out the first ball. But half an hour beyond scheduled start time, she still had not appeared. By then most of the Flags were in uniform and ready to play, and Bull was into a routine tantrum with the umps regarding rules and regulations applicable to changing the lineup before play had actually begun.

Exactly an hour and seventeen minutes late, the Congresswoman arrived. She had been delayed at the gate by a protest group called "WOUAL" (Washington Owes Us a Living). Thinking there might be some votes there, she gave them a lengthy speech that finally wore them down.

Then, after a brief introduction in the ballpark and total silence from the crowd, she shot-putted the ball somewhat toward home plate. The catcher diplomatically charged out toward the mound to retrieve the ball and strode the remaining ten feet to shake her hand.

The game finally began.

Homer got to bat in the first inning – with the Flags leading 3 to 0 – and barely made it to first on a Texas leaguer to left field. But he was thrown out at second on the next play, long after the next hitter had crossed first base. Otherwise, his only in-the-game mishap was in the fourth inning when he was tagged out between third and home on a bases loaded single (would have been an easy double) by Jose. Bull was in apoplexy.

Homer went on to collect two more singles along with four intentional walks in what turned out to be the longest game of the season for the hard-charging Baltimore Flags. Although actual playing time was not unusual, each manager was required to file a 23-page report at the end of each inning, plus appendixes justifying each time the manager or a coach had communicated with a player.

By the seventh inning stretch the game had gone well past midnight. Homer had concluded that it must be bedtime, so he showered, dressed, and caught a taxi back to his luxury pad overlooking the Baltimore Inner Harbor.

In spite of Homer's absence those last two innings, the Flags went on to win that first game in Washington 11 to 9.

But they did not win the following evening. Homer had been suspended for the last two games of that Washington series. And the Bureaucrats won that second game 3 to 2. That game also went past midnight, as did the third game that was finally called in the top of the eleventh with the score tied 2 to 2. Since it was half-past four, and the Flags needed to get on the road for a three-game series in New York, the two clubs agreed to finish this game next time they were to meet in Washington.

Homer had been watching the game on TV from his comfy pad in Baltimore, but he'd dozed off in the sixth inning and hadn't heard the outcome until the morning news. Baltimore had escaped Washington one win, one loss, and one delay.

Homer managed to join the team on the trip to New York but things were tenuous. This last incident had brought things to a head. Bull was adamant with Flags' management. "Either you outright release that dimwit," or "at least put him on the first bus to the minors." Even the media seemed to be sympathetic with Bull's case: "Homer's Dumb-out" was the lead headline in the *Sun* next day. And the TV reporters were espousing several theories about this strange phenomenon, Homer.

This latest controversy only spurred fan interest to new heights, leaving Flags' management in a quandary. Well, not really. "Bull, either you learn to live with Homer as he is, or we'll have to find a new manager," which was a gamble on their part. For under no circumstances could they afford to lose either half of the equation.

Bull stayed.

His only consolation was that Flags' management agreed to a technicality which would deprive Homer of any opportunity to be selected as DH for the All Star game in July. They would remove him as a candidate for the game; then reinstate him after the All Star game.

This satisfied Bull's immediate vengeance. And it didn't really bother Homer, once it was explained to him. He didn't understand what the All Star furor was all about anyway. And it would give him two or three days to go back to New Somerton and see his folks, and Rover, and maybe some of his friends.

As for Flags' management, it was a painful concession, considering the publicity opportunity of Homer still batting 1000, in the Air Star game. The fans would have gone ballistic.

By mid-season the Flags had gone on two brilliant winning streaks, having won 19 straight road games at one point, and were at an enviable record of 61 wins and 14 losses by the All Star game break.

They were on a tear. The team was breaking all kinds of records, not the least of which was attendance. Well, actually, if Homer's statistics were extracted from the team totals, they weren't breaking all that many records on the field.

In fact, only two Flags had made the All Star Team: Marty Angels, by a narrowest of vote margins, as a relief pitcher, and Jose was picked as a backup infielder but would not be starting. Homer's name, of course, was not on the ballot per the earlier agreement between Flags' management and Bull.

But Homer was breaking all kinds of records: force-outs at second base, tag-outs while base running, and errors per inning played on defense (not many). But then there was the other side of it: at 23 home runs he was second in the league, at 82 doubles and 129 singles he was league leader, as he was at 199 RBIs. And Homer was still batting 1000. He had also drawn an all-time major league record of 155 intentional walks, plus 46 un-intentional, and had been hit-by-pitched balls 21 times.

"The Enigma of Baseball" one national sports weekly described him. "Utterly Useless at Every Task in Baseball (Except Hitting the Ball)." And what they might have added: "In Pumping Up Sports Media Advertising Dollars."

But if Homer had become a goldmine to Baltimore, to baseball, and to the media, the Bull-Homer story had become platinum. It seems that a talented young Baltimore cartoonist had syndicated a weekly series featuring "The Antics of Bull and Homer." 189 daily newspapers around the country quickly signed up. Subscriptions soared. People who had never been to a baseball game were in total combat at newsstands for copies.

One cartoon showed Bull holding Homer upside down at home plate as Homer whacks the ball over the center field wall for an upside down home run. Another showed Homer running the wrong direction from first base to home plate, bumping shoulders with the hitter who was attempting to run from home to first, as the ump is signaling both runners out, while the entire Flags' bench is holding Bull down in the dugout as the team physician pours a number 10 can of sedatives down his gullet. And on they came, and on came the public after them.

Jose had offered to get All Star game tickets for Homer and his parents but Homer needed a break. He just wanted to go back to New Somerton and relax. So as Bull, along with Flags' management and a contingent of players, headed off for the game in Pittsburgh, Homer headed off for his six-hour drive. To try to get to New Somerton by air would have been just too big a hassle. And even with two speeding tickets, Homer figured he came out ahead.

Somehow Homer forgot to watch the All Star game on TV that night. However, he had gone back into Marietta to visit the old batting practice cage where his baseball career had begun. But it was gone; ground under the foundation of a new mini-mall under construction at the site.

The regular season resumed with an overwhelming performance by the Flags. They won 31 straight games, another major league record. And as baseball technicians were relentless in their needling of Bull, it was observed that Homer's hitting had accounted for the margin of victory in every one of those 31 games.

The Flags swept not only the despised Capitalists, the disgusting Lawyers, the inept Bureaucrats, the pathetic Socialists, and all of the International Universe league teams, but they "whumped" Arizona, Denver, St. Louis, and Florida as well.

And the most remarkable thing of all was that Homer and Bull had been at peace for a record nine consecutive weeks. And Homer was still batting 1000.

# CHAPTER SIXTEEN

## *Wilmington – Early July*

It was a hot summer weekend. For me, Sunday mornings were no different from any other morning. I'd come down and sit on the top step at my end of the stoop and watch people go by.

On weekdays I was never down there early enough to see people headed for work, or kids for school. But on Sundays people heading to and from church would go by at all different times.

Now that summer school was on, only days I'd ever see Arsha and Bibbie were Saturday and Sunday. They'd show up around 9 a.m. or 9:30, fool around for half an hour, go back up to the apartment, then half hour later, they'd be back down and stay for another hour or so. It was getting so I was happy to see them. During the week days I kind of missed their company now.

Arsha was usually a little quiet at first. She'd seem to be just thinking to herself a lot. She'd take short, slow walks by herself. Then, sometimes she'd come back and ask me a bunch of questions about anything and everything. When I'd first moved in, it used to piss me off some. I'd give her short answers like "I don't know." Sometimes I wouldn't even answer her. But now I was beginning to try to answer her best I could.

By late morning on the weekend, Bandi, or some other kid, would usually show up and they'd walk and talk and play jump rope and the like.

Bibbie would usually putter around down on the concrete the other side of the stoop. He'd seemed to find a hundred different things to keep him busy: sticks, pebbles, bugs, and broken pieces of this or that. Every once in a while he'd pick something up and try to show it to me. At first I used to just ignore him. But over time I'd gotten more attached to the little bastard. Now he'd hold up a broken windshield wiper to show me and I'd smile and nod and tell him "That's really something." He'd smile and giggle and shake it at me. Then he'd explain it all to me as either "wa, wa, wa" or "ba, ba, ba." I'd nod and tell him that he was "right on." Then he'd look at it all bug eyed and turn around and go looking for something else.

Fifth of July Sunday was a little more quiet than most. Lot of people must have gone away or something. But Arsha and Bibbie and me – we went pretty much through our same routine.

They were down front for the second time that morning. Bandi must have been a little later showing up than usual. I could tell Arsha was getting a little bored. She seemed like she had something on her mind but didn't quite know how to say it.

"Mister?" Then she paused.

"Yeah. What's up?"

"Mister," she took another long pause, "did you have fun at the carnival the other night?"

"Yeah, I did. Hope you did."

"I really did!" She was burstin' with enthusiasm. "So did Bandi! We really had a fun time!"

"That's great," I said.

"Well you know what?" She came right back.

"What's that?"

"My mother said that it would be okay if you were going again that we could go with you."

I had a moment to think. "Who the hell does the *bitch* think she is?" Then I wondered a moment. "Who the hell does Arsha think she is? This little brat is beginning to manipulate me, and I've been letting her do it. Screw this."

"Don't plan to go again."

"Well it is still going on 'til Monday night." She wasn't giving up.

I didn't say anything.

"Wouldn't you like to take Bibbie on the merry-go-round again, Mister?"

"This kid's gonna be dangerous when she gets older," I thought. "Damn!"

"Maybe," I let slip. Why couldn't I've just kept my mouth shut? She's got me. Damn it.

I'll back off I figured. "But not this year."

That stopped her. Then I saw Bandi coming up in the distance.

"That Bandi coming?" Lucky break. Thank God for Bandi. That distracted Arsha just long enough that I was able to get up and head upstairs to the apartment.

"See you after a bit," I mumbled as I closed the screen door behind me.

Half hour later I came back down. The three of them were still playing. Arsha came over toward me.

"Mister?" She'd hardly gotten that out of her mouth when I heard the *bitch* come charging down the stairs. She threw the screen door open like a damned tornado.

"What time will you be home, Mom?" Arsha called quickly after her mother, who by that time was five yards down the sidewalk.

"6 o'clock," she answered real blunt like and kept right on walking. The way she was dressed I guessed she must be headed for work.

"What can we have for lunch?" Arsha called as she followed after her mother close enough so as her mother could at least hear her.

"Crackers."

I could barely hear her answer, as by that time she was a ways down the sidewalk, and walking high speed.

"Crackers. For Chrissakes. That's what she left those two kids for lunch? Son-of-a-bitch. What a miserable, rotten *bitch*. Crackers."

I had to fight it back to keep the kids from hearing me.

In a half fit of anger, I blurted out, "What about we all go over to the park for a bit? Maybe I'll get you a hot dog for lunch."

As we were crossing the street toward the park entrance, I decided to do this a little more interesting than usual: "Arsha, I'm gonna take Bibbie and go all the way 'round the bike path. It'll probably take us a while. You want to come with us?" I fully expected her to say no. She and Bandi would probably want to go off the other direction to the swing sets. Be damned, she said, "Yes."

We worked our way 'round the path, through the woods with all the big trees and shrubs. I loved it – the little brook running along down below us.

Bibbie trundled along at his own pace, checking out all the exciting things he saw along the way. We were in no hurry.

The girls went on ahead until they got to the hot dog stand. He must'a opened up for the weekend.

Once we finished there, the girls went on ahead, but I made them stay in sight. I'd carry Bibbie a while, then he'd trundle a while, then I'd carry a while, then he'd trundle some more. We were just having a relaxing good old time.

The girls were good about staying in sight. Every once in a while I'd have to scoop Bibbie up to let bikes or joggers go by.

We were getting up into a part of the park we'd never seen before. The girls had spotted a kids' zoo up off to the left on the other side of the brook. They'd walked across a little footbridge to go see it, so Bibbie and I followed along.

By the time we caught up, the zoo attendant was talking to the girls. She seemed to be explaining about the baby goats they were checking out. She was being very helpful, answering all their questions, more patient than I would of.

Bibbie was beside himself. He got all excited when two little monkeys came scrambling over and peaked out of their cage right at him. He was giggling and shaking his arms and explaining "wa, wa" and "ba, ba" to them. And they'd just look at him and scratch themselves and then he'd try to talk to them some more.

We'd looked at a few more animals, then Bibbie saw a squirrel hopping across a brick terrace area along one corner of the zoo. There were benches and tables, all looking out over the brook and a sort of terraced area with some flower beds. Looked like a good spot to rest for a moment, so I followed Bibbie as he headed for the squirrel.

The girls were already there, just fooling around. I asked them if they'd watch Bibbie while I checked out the men's room I'd seen on the other side of the zoo building.

But when I got back a few minutes later, they weren't there. And they weren't around the corner along the other side of the zoo.

"Where in the hell are they?" I made my way back 'round the building toward the entrance to the women's rest room. A young mother was coming out with her baby in arm.

"You didn't see a couple of girls in there with a baby brother, did you?"

"No, I didn't," she answered me very courteously, paused a moment, and looked at me as though she'd like to help. But I was stumped, so I just thanked her and headed on around the building. "Where in the hell could they be?" I was mumbling to myself, half frustrated, half worried.

"God damn it! Where are they?"

Then I looked way up the path, the direction we'd been headed before the zoo. Sure as hell, there was Arsha and Bandi up there b-s'ing with some other kids about their age.

"They must have dragged Bibbie up there with them." I couldn't see much below their shoulders because of a large rock this side of the path blocking my view. They probably couldn't of heard me if I'd tried to yell at them, so I slowly made my way across the bridge and up onto the path. By that point I could see them clearly enough -- but no Bibbie. "Where the hell is he?"

"If they let him get down there playing in the dirt, I'm gonna give those two holy hell. Damn it."

"Arsha! Where's Bibbie?" I called soon as I'd gotten fairly close.

She turned 'round toward me and paused a few seconds.

"Over by the zoo."

"Holy shit. They didn't just go off and leave him all alone, did they?"

"We told him to stay there and wait for you," she pleaded.

The little bastard was nowhere in sight. The zoo attendant hadn't seen him. Although she came right over to offer help as soon as she realized what we were all upset about. The woman with the baby, who'd come out of the restroom earlier, hadn't seen him. We asked a couple other people we'd seen looking at the zoo when we were. They hadn't seen him.

"Jesus Christ! Where is he?"

I was panicked! Arsha started half sobbing. She started frantically looking all over, calling out, "Bibbie, Bibbie!"

Things were flashing through my head. The brook wasn't deep enough for him to drown; even if he fell down in it. At least it'd be tough to drown – I thought. It's just a trickle. "God! Nobody would kidnap him, would they?"

I could barely see through the trees the rows of two-story apartment buildings across a street which ran along the park way off to the left of the zoo area. It looked kind of run down. But it was too hard to see it real well.

"Jesus Christ. Every month or so you'd hear about some child getting abducted."

Arsha and Bandi were off searching through some shrubs down the bank behind the zoo. The zoo attendant was on her cell phone. The mother with the baby had explained things to a couple of other women.

They looked like they were combing the woods toward that street over toward those apartment buildings.

I was switching from sickening fear that he'd fallen in somewhere we couldn't see him to "I'll kill anybody who'd tried to abduct him!" While the others were out searching, I was near frozen trying to think of the possibilities.

The zoo attendant came over. "I've called the police. They'll be here in a few minutes."

I was going berserk. Could some zoo animal somewhere have gotten hold of him – and dragged him into their den? Is there an open manhole near here? Are some fucking teenagers doing something to him?" Crazy ideas, just crazy! I was limping around, here, then there, zigzagging all over the area surrounding the zoo.

Arsha was way over in some trees sobbing and gasping and screaming for him!

A couple cops came hurrying down the path from the way we'd come. The zoo attendant quickly briefed them and they set out searching. Then way off up straight ahead through the woods, two more cops, a man and a woman, were coming prowling through the woods toward us.

All of a sudden they stopped. The one started talking on her phone. Then just as sudden, they turned and started scrambling up the slope through the woods to their right, kind of toward the street running between the park and those apartments.

"They're on to something," I muttered.

A path wound up the slope from the zoo area – up through the woods to the far corner of the park up ahead. They hit the path running on up out of sight.

Next thing I see the other two cops come running across the brook and up through the woods after them.

"Christ, I hope they found Bibbie. And that he's okay." I was praying.

A cluster of us were all gathered by the rail running along the edge of the pavement 'round the zoo. We were all looking and straining – up toward where the cops ran.

Arsha hurried 'round front of me and looked up at me. "What are they doing, Mister? Did they find Bibbie? Huh?"

"Not yet. I don't know. Maybe." My eyes were glued toward those woods. It was forever. Then I thought I saw a cop, or somebody coming down the path way off through the trees. It's a cop. I saw him through a little clearing. Then another cop. "Oh my God!" It was the woman cop, carrying Bibbie! And he looked okay, best I could see at that distance. "Oh, thank God!"

Then came the other two cops, one pulling a little red wagon. "What the hell's that all about?"

The lead cop was on his phone talking as they got closer. Arsha and me started up the path to meet them. He was okay, all right. We could see his little legs kicking lazily, and his hand pulling on her arm insignia. And she was saying something to him every few feet.

"Thank God!"

"Is this your youngster, sir?" The lead cop could see our urgency from several yards away.

"He sure is, Officer!" I was bellowing with relief. Arsha ran ahead babbling happy scoldings to her little brother.

It was damned clear to the cops, the way Bibbie was clammering for us, that he belonged to us. But we had to go through the ID check:

name, address, phone number, etc. Then Bibbie's full name – holy shit, I paused. Thank God Arsha was there. Then they had to know our connection with Bibbie – both of us. After a long phone discussion back with his headquarters, he explained that they could only release the boy to a parent.

So up the path we followed the cops to their patrol wagon. They loaded Bibbie, Arsha, Bandi, and me all into the back and off we went for home. I'd explained that Bibbie's mother wouldn't be back 'til six, but they were following procedures, and taking this one step at a time.

Bibbie had taken all this in stride. We teased him and tickled him, and he giggled half the trip back. Arsha took the woman cop up to their apartment. They came back down shortly, and after a lot of discussion and another phone call, they decided that she would stay with Bibbie until his mother showed up and her partner took off. My gut feel was they were bending the rules, but that was all fine with Arsha and me. We had Bibbie back.

After about an hour, the *bitch* did show up when she said she would. Her face was in panic when she first saw the cop. Probably some guilt panic I figured. But she settled down when it was all explained. We all had to go up to their apartment for a half hour, to verify everything to the cop, before she could leave, and so could I.

While we'd been waiting for the *bitch* to show up, the cop explained to us what had happened: About the time the zoo attendant had called to report that Bibbie was missing, a woman had been waiting at the bus stop there at the far corner of the park. She'd noticed a couple of boys, 10 or 11 years old, she said, racing up the park path pulling a screaming baby in a wagon. She thought they were acting strange, laughing and trash talking and the like. So when they got up to where the park path met the sidewalk by the bus stop, she'd confronted them. They'd quickly taken off down the street, leaving the wagon and Bibbie, as it had turned out, just sitting there. She'd gotten a man with a cell phone – apparently he'd been there waiting for the bus too – to call 911. The police were quickly able to match that call up with the zoo attendant's and that's how it all got put together.

They'd figured the boys had stolen the wagon somewhere and were just up to some boy brat prank. Exactly where they'd gotten hold of Bibbie wasn't clear, but they'd had to have been prowling around the zoo area just looking for some mischief to get into.

I'd have loved to have gotten my hands on the little creeps. But that was water over the dam. "Fucking scum brats."

In spite of some heavy fireworks shooting from the park area, I slept damn good that night.

# CHAPTER SEVENTEEN

# *Wilmington – Early July*

Next morning I felt great. I was relieved and relaxed. I'd even reconsidered Arsha's earlier pestering.

"Arsha. 'Member ya asked me 'bout going back to the carnival 'gain tonight?"

"Yes," she answered me sorta hesitating.

"Still want to go?"

"I'm going with Bandi and her mother." We both paused a minute. "I thought you didn't want to take us. So Bandi asked her mother. And they're picking me up."

"Well, damn," I thought. "That leaves Bibbie and me stood up," I chuckled. I don't think she understood, "stood up."

"Well you can still go, Mister," she pleaded.

"How 'bout Bibbie?" I was just sorta teasing her. But it was always hard to get one up with Arsha.

"I'll ask my mother if you can take him too." Thank God Arsha was always there to deal with her mother. 'Cause I sure as hell wasn't gonna.

That evening Bibbie and me went trudging and trundling down the alley to the carnival. It was kinda neat to see the lights of the carnival, and hear the music, all in the distance as we got closer and closer.

But once we got there, I didn't have Arsha to explain to me what Bibbie was trying to say with his "wa, wa" and "ba, ba." So I had to guess. I knew he liked ice cream so I got him a cone at the ice cream tent we'd come to as soon as we'd entered. What a mess. It took me 10 minutes and 25 paper napkins to get it off his hands and his face. And he was still all sticky as hell. I never did get it off his shirt. But he'd loved every lick of it. "Little bastard," I chuckled to myself. Then I knew for sure he'd want to go on the merry-go-round, so we headed that direction.

On the way over there we passed down by all the tents where they play the games for prizes, including the ring toss with the teddy bear Arsha had pestered me about the first night. So just on a lark I thought I'd give it one try to win Bibbie a teddy bear.

"Three rings for a dollar!" the guy was yelling.

I paid him the buck and just barely missed with the first ring. I was trying to hold Bibbie's hand – he was pulling and tugging 'cause at ground level he couldn't see the action.

By heavens, the second ring dropped right on! "We won a teddy bear, Bibbie!" When I first put it in his arms, he gave a big grin. Then he stroked it a couple times. Then he did an excited little dance and giggle. Then he dropped it on the ground; little bastard. But he picked it up and looked all stern; like he was faking it. I picked him up. He squeezed the teddy up close to his chest and off we went to the merry-go-round. He was just as excited as the first time we rode it the other night. And I still warmed a little hearing that old time music as we went round and round.

I thought I saw Arsha and Bandi as we rounded past the concession tents on one loop. And as Bibbie and me got off at the end of the ride, sure enough, they were back toward the end of the ticket line for the next ride.

Arsha spotted the teddy bear. "Where'd you get that, Bibbie? Where'd you get that?" She was half agitated. "Where'd Bibbie get that teddy bear, Mister?"

"At the ring toss where we were the other night – except this time I ringed it." She started to pout, stomped her foot, and turned toward Bandi.

"Look, I was lucky Arsha." I was pleading. What the hell am I doing pleading to that damn kid? "I'll go try to win you one."

The two women – one I figured was probably Bandi's mother – were nudging the girls along in line so I just nodded and smiled.

"See you back home, Arsh'. I'll try to bring you a teddy." I didn't even try. I'd figured the odds of doing it again were zero. I remember as a kid I'd never won anything on one of those games. "She'll get over it."

I toted Bibbie around through the crowds a little while. He clammered for a cotton candy, but that was more than I could deal with. That goddamn sticky stuff all over everything. He didn't show any interest in any other rides, thank God. After a bit, we were both getting a little tired. So after a long, dragged out visit to porta toilet, we slowly headed back across the park toward home.

Not having to fool with Arsha and Bandi, this time was only half as long as the first evening. But I think ol' Bibbie enjoyed it. "Little bastard."

It was too dark for him to toddle-walk much of the way. So I had to tote him the whole trip. He dropped his teddy a few times. I'd grumble and swear lightly, put him down for a moment until we got teddy, then lift up again, and limp

on.

## CHAPTER EIGHTEEN

# *New York – Late July*

"Da bus leaves in two minutes – widja or wid oud-ja," the bus driver shouted. The bus taking the team from La Guardia Airport to their hotel left in two minutes – without Homer and Budge Ziff. Budge, an outfielder, always seemed to have a chip on his shoulder, and he wasn't about to be rushed by some New York bus driver. So he wasn't.

Now Budge, had he been listening, should have been able to get Homer and himself to the hotel by taxi. After all, he'd been to New York with the team several times before. But instead, he got them to the hotel where the team used to stay. An hour later, and two phone calls to Baltimore to find out just where they were supposed to be, Homer and Budge loaded into another taxi.

That the driver didn't speak English was only part of the problem. That he'd been in New York only a week was even bigger. During the two and a half hours it took him to find the hotel he was the target of great verbal abuse from Budge. So that by the time they had actually arrived the two were not on speaking terms.

"You pay him," was Budge's curt instruction to Homer. Budge bolted into the hotel in a huff. Homer, entirely bewildered by the whole episode, pulled a hundred dollar bill from his clip and handed it to the driver who abruptly jumped into his taxi and burned rubber.

Homer had always been taught not to tell on others for their mistakes – that they should 'fess-up on their own. And he surely hoped Budge would 'fess-up: for he was mortified at what weaponry Bull might use on him over missing the team bus.

Well, Budge did not 'fess-up. In fact, as became clearer later – or at least as anything was ever clear to Homer – Budge had quietly implied that the whole bus-taxi incident was Homer's screw-up.

But, for the moment, as the team arrived at Capitalist Stadium, Homer was greatly relieved that Bull was preoccupied with another matter. Trivial as it seemed, the Capitalists' management had instituted a requirement that each player on a visiting team had to buy a full admissions box seat ticket in order to be allowed to play in Capitalist Stadium. Bull was in a near trance. By the time the team physician had gotten him settled down, the Flags' management had paid for the tickets and everybody was in the clubhouse getting changed.

Everybody but Homer, that was. Homer had misunderstood. Thinking that he had to go get in line at the ticket booth to buy his box seat, he was out there waiting his turn – several people had jumped the line while he was waiting. Half an hour later Jose's instincts led him out to retrieve Homer from the line before Bull had gotten wind of this one.

Homer wasn't surprised that his name was not on the line-up Bull handed the umpire before the game. But he did scratch his head once when Budge Ziff's name was announced as starting in left field. Budge struck out four times in the game, and the Flags lost 8 to 0.

Back at the hotel that evening an additional aggravation began to circulate. For not only had the Capitalists' management required that each Flags player purchase a game ticket, but scuttlebutt now had it that the visiting team was required to buy a $5,000 insurance policy per player for each game played in historic Capitalist Stadium.

Bull decided this was management's problem. And Homer agreed with him, much to Bull's comfort. The Flags had enough to do just trying to win ball games. And they did. They absolutely "whumped" the Capitalists, as Homer explained it to a *Sun* reporter. The Flags took the next three games 7 to 5, 5 to 0, and 10 to 3. Homer went seven-for-seven with two home runs, three bases-on-balls, and was twice hit by pitched balls.

No other pitching staff in baseball would now have tried to pitch to Homer on as many as seven occasions, but the arrogance of the Capitalist bullpen simply would not allow otherwise. Besides, it had become a challenge to pitch to Homer. "Some pitcher, some team, somehow is going to find some way to get Homer out," according to the *Daily News*.

The Baltimore media traveling on the team's trips had pretty much divided up the labor, half following Bull and the other half tagging around with Homer. Each group had its' own challenge. Bull was tougher to pry information from, while Homer had very little to pry. But that mattered little to the ecstatic fans back in Baltimore. If Homer's only statement was "Reckon that's right," it was exciting news to loyal Flags fans.

Next stop, Confederate Field, and a three-game series with the beleaguered Atlanta Confederates who were sporting a 16-game losing streak. The Flags extended that to 19, remaining solidly in first place in the Eastern Division.

As the team bus had pulled into the stadium late that afternoon, Homer had noticed a large crowd, cordoned off by the police, over in one corner of the parking lot. He didn't learn until reading a full-page spread in the *Atlanta Constitution Journal* next morning describing an extended family, all 271 of them, of rednecks who'd gathered for an outing. As it turned out, they'd been able to pool only enough money to buy two tickets to a game. So in an expression of democracy, they'd set up a tournament whereby the two finalists would earn the tickets.

The tournament was a dead squirrel pitching contest – much like horseshoe – whereby stacks of four old truck tires formed targets into which the dead squirrels must be pitched from one hundred feet.

Since none were wearing shoes, it had been simple enough to pick the redneck with the largest feet to step off the hundred. And that had presented no problems as they'd recruited some local kid passing by who could count all the way to one hundred for them.

But in the 32 hours they'd been there, they had encountered another problem that had resulted in the police presence. Apparently some local fans had objected to the idea that the stacks of tires were doubling as restroom facilities. The rednecks hadn't understood the function of the portable toilets aligning one side of the parking lot, so they'd set up their own.

That mess, and all the dead squirrels, had created an unfortunate furor. And, although they'd managed to complete the tournament, in the end the two winners were turned away from the turnstiles for lack of shoes. So by the time the police and the sanitation department had cleaned everything away, the media, in their glee, had missed the first half of the ballgame.

The Flags had arrived in Atlanta amidst another great turmoil. The city had sued the ball club to change its nickname on the grounds that it was costing Atlanta millions of dollars in lost convention business. The

Confederates' management contended that since the stadium was filled every game, in spite of the dismal won-loss record, that somebody must think the name "Confederate" was okay.

The media had been able to whip up a frenzy, and the lawsuit had gotten downright nasty. Club management had threatened to sell the franchise to a telecommunications entrepreneur, Bill Sherman, who had proposed to change the name to the "Carpet Baggers." The incensed fans had called a two-game strike during which nobody attended, or risked attending, a game. The city had temporarily backed off its position the day before the series with Baltimore, so the stadium was packed as the Flags took the field that evening.

By the end of the series, Homer had gone three for three against the Confederates pitching and was walked eleven times (was forced out at second four of those times). Only one Atlanta pitcher had tried to hit him with a pitch. But Homer had developed great skill at anticipating and ducking such attempts by aggressive pitchers, which were increasing as the season wore on.

While in Atlanta, CNN had hoped to invite Homer as their guest on a morning talk show with world wide coverage. But Bull abruptly cancelled the interview, requiring Homer to spend the morning at "base running" practice. It didn't bother Homer much. But CNN retaliated by running a 15-minute caricature of "Baltimore's Juvenile Manager," showing video clips of numerous emotional explosions Bull had been caught at over the years.

Fortunately, it didn't run until the Flags were on their way out of town so Bull didn't actually see it. He did hear a lot about it later. But even Bull's ire was held at bay by the incredibly successful season the Flags were having. And Homer was still batting 1000.

# CHAPTER NINETEEN

## *Baltimore - Early August*

The next four games back at Ripken Field were sort of a harbinger of heaven to Flags' fans. They "whumped" the San Francisco Fogs four straight. Homer went 8 for 8 with two homeruns, two doubles, and four singles with 11 RBIs. He also collected 17 intentional walks and was hit twice by pitched balls.

The Baltimore media were ecstatic. Advertising revenues were at records. And all TV talk shows had been replaced with specials featuring the various Flags' players, Bull, the coaches, Angelo Peters, the bat boy, ball girls, and the grounds crew. Channel 483 featured the weekly Homer and Bull Show or the Bull and Homer Show on those alternate weeks Bull was on. (Otherwise he refused to appear).

The Flags were now eight and a half games up on the second place New York Capitalists. And some old time Baltimore fans still contended doggedly that second priority was to win the World Series; first, to go undefeated against the Capitalists.

Every game for the rest of the season was sold out. Scalpers were getting $100 for a pair of left field upper deck seats. Even more striking was that virtually all seats held by season ticket holders were actually filled at the games.

The Fogs batters seemed mesmerized by it all. They lived down to their name by striking out a record 79 times in the four games, collecting only four hits and three runs in the series. "They simply stood there and watched the pitches go by," according to the *Sun*. "They swung their bats as though they were in some mist," according to the *San Francisco Examiner*.

Actually, the only runs the Flags scored in the four games were on Homer's eleven RBIs plus the two he personally scored on a couple of two-run home runs hit by Jose and Bailey Clark. And these 13 runs were enough to sweep the series.

But Bull was unimpressed. In fact he was in his usual furor over Homer's ineptitude. Although he had hit a home run, two singles, and a double in the first game, it had been a seriously flawed performance according to Bull. "He couldn't lay down a bunt if the season depended on it!" Bull had screamed. "He'll stand there holding the bat in the dumbest awkward bunting stance imaginable! Then he'll take a strike or two! Then he hauls off and swings like hell at the next pitch!"

This was all true. And when he swung at that next pitch, he'd sent the ball into the far corner of center field, scoring the runner from first, and even making it all the way into second himself. "But that isn't what we signaled him to do!" Bull shouted at Hank. Throughout the season Hank had worked patiently with Homer on the fundamentals of bunting, but it hadn't taken. And Bull was miffed.

As the inning had ended on the next out, and Homer was slowly finding his way back to the dugout, Bull could not contain himself. He went charging out to confront Homer. "You dumb …!" In his anger he turned his head to spat out a huge wad of tobacco juice. But a healthy breeze sent a portion of it right into Homer's face. Even Bull was at a momentary loss for words. Homer was petrified. As Bull stomped off, Homer slunk slowly into his corner of the dugout, towel to face. Homer wished he were home with Rover.

In addition to his inability to follow Bull's signals and instructions, Homer would frequently grab the wrong bat, en route to the on-deck circle, when it was his turn. His teammates had gotten used to it and forgave him for the most part. But from time-to-time he'd forget to step into the on-deck circle, wandering over to the fence to chat with any fan who tried shouting a question at him. Either Hank or Bull had always caught it in time to motion him back to the circle before an ump picked up on it. But it was one more aggravation to Bull.

Just prior to the fourth game of the San Francisco series, *Baseball Weekly* had done a full-length feature article on Homer. It commented on the phenomenal impact Homer's hitting had had on baseball in Baltimore, on his relationship with Bull, and on his record breaking statistics. It observed that if one were to extract the runs Homer had accounted for to–date, the Flags would be in next to last place in the Eastern Division.

# CHAPTER TWENTY

# *Wilmington – Early September*

I didn't see Bibbie or Arsha much that first week of the new school year. Just a couple of times out front after Arsha had come home from school.

I'd been down to the grocery one afternoon and just as I'd turned the corner to come up our street, I'd seen the *bitch* carrying Bibbie up the front steps and into the house. From a distance it looked like he was laying his head on her shoulder. I thought I even saw her pat him lightly on the fanny; as though she might actually love him. "Damn."

I'd learned from Arsha who was babysitting him while Arsha was at school.

"Arsha, who takes care of Bibbie when you're not here? I mean your mother's at work and all?"

"Well, she doesn't go to work 'til lunch time. So Dack watches Bibbie 'til I get home."

"Christ! She trusts that scum ball to take care of him," I thought. "God damn. I can't believe it!" I knew Arsha got home about 3 p.m. so Bibbie, poor little bastard, is stuck with Dack for three hours. Except that I suspected that Dack wasn't even around half the time. Maybe that was better anyway. "Damn!"

That Saturday morning was one of those great, late summer days. Arsha and Bibbie were already out front when I got down there. And Bandi showed up about the same time as I did.

"You kids want to go to the park this morning?"

"Bandi and I have to go to school this morning to practice dance." She seemed pretty bubbly and enthused about it.

"Oh, you do?"

"Yes! We're going to be in a show. And we have to practice all morning," she explained all proud and excited.

So Bibbie and me went limping off to the park. Just us two.

I was carrying him across the street to the park entrance when a family started to get into their car parked in the first slot next to where we stepped up onto the sidewalk. The parents were maybe in their late 20's, fatter than hell, both of them. The dad looked kinda pissed about something. The mom put the little girl into the back seat on the curb side and got herself into the front seat passenger side. All of a sudden, the dad picks the little boy up, swings him around the trunk into the car, jerks the rear door open, and slams the kid right into the back seat! God damn, I thought he'd killed him.

He slammed the car door and bolted into the driver's seat. By this time the mother was sobbing sorta quietly it looked.

I didn't have a real good angle but best I could see the kid was okay. He'd looked stunned at first, then winced, then seemed to be trying to fight back tears.

What a prick! If I'd been younger and not half broken, I'd have grabbed the SOB and done the same to him.

As they roared off, I thought what a life that kid has to live. And his poor goddamn mother was probably too scared to say boo.

The whole thing shook me up so much Bibbie and me didn't stay long that day. We puttered around the nearest park bench along side the bike path. I was still fuming a half-hour later. Wasn't really in the mood for more than that. So I picked the little bastard up and started back home.

September 15 came, the day for me to move down to my new apartment on the first floor. I'd sure as hell been looking forward to it. It had been a pain, dragging up and down that narrow staircase all the time; especially when I was tired.

That weird SOB had moved out the day before. Mrs. Kline had dropped the keys off late that afternoon. She'd explained to me something about the latch on the back window and some other tips about the refrigerator and the tricky door lock. I spent the whole morning toting my stuff down the stairs – up and down, up and down.

Early-on the *bitch* had come charging out the door, on her way to work. From then on I didn't hear a peep out of their apartment all day 'til Arsha got home. At first I didn't think much about it, that I never heard any sound at all as I'd passed by the door to their second floor apartment, but by midmorning I'd begun to wonder. "Awfully quiet in there." You'd think with a toddler in there you'd hear something, sometime. Only time I'd ever heard Dack say anything was from a distance; when once in a while he and the *bitch* would be in a screaming match. Otherwise, his eyes always half-dazed, straight ahead, he looked like he was under sedative. Then I started to wonder. "Considerin' the kind of asshole he seems to be, you don't suppose he gives Bibbie a sedative of some kind? You know, just to make babysittin' easy. I wouldn't put it past that creep."

Then I began to think about how little I'd seen of Bibbie since this babysitting had started. And how drowsy he'd looked a lot of the time when I had seen him. That was usually after Arsha'd gotten home from school and brought him out front to play. "That grungy jerk. I wouldn't put it past him."

At least I was carrying stuff down the stairs and not up. When I'd first moved in here, Jack, one of my buddies from where I'd worked, had moved me down here in his pickup truck. He'd done most of the carrying up the stairs to the third floor.

But now I'd lost contact with everybody – it's a damned pain to be disabled - even just partly so. Anyway, what the hell else do I have to do with my time? No point in pissing and moaning about it.

"Mister, are you all moved yet?" It was Arsha. She'd sneaked up behind me halfway up the stairs on one of my last trips in the move.

"Just about, Arsh, just about." I was kinda happy to hear her cheerful little voice.

I'd finished moving in by 'round half past three. Down the stairs came Arsha with Bibbie; as usual, half carrying, half dragging.

He seemed out of it. But also a little cranky. And he kept getting crankier as the afternoon wore on. I could hear them out my open front window. Hadn't been able to hear all the commotions up on the third floor. I wondered if she'd always scolded him like that. Bandi had showed up, as usual, and I guess he was getting in their way – whatever they were doing.

"Bibbie, stop it!" 'bout a dozen times before I finally wandered out to see if I could put a stop to it. Goddamn kids could be a nuisance.

I tried to distract him. Tried to get him to come over to me to play sticks or something. Get him out of their hair. At least so Arsha would stop her damned bitching at him. Getting on my nerves. Then I noticed he had bruises all up one side. Jesus, they were bad! No wonder he was cranky.

"Arsha, what happened to him – these bruises?"

"He fell down." She kept on playing some game with Bandi.

"How'd he fall, where was that?"

"I don't know. Dack just said he fell." She kept on playing.

I gotta talk with Mrs. Kline when she comes up here tomorrow to get my old keys. I've got to find out what agency to call. I can't take this much longer. I wished to fuck that scumball Dack would get hit by a car or somethin'! God damn!!

## CHAPTER TWENTY-ONE

# *Baltimore – Early September*

The Flags were now starting into their longest home stand of the season. Up next, the Chicago Wind Chills. Homer's parents had made the six-hour drive from New Somerton to take in all three games.

The Flags won all three. In addition, his parents were treated to another Homer performance: four-for-four including a home run, a triple, a double, and a single, six RBIs; nine intentional walks; and only one hit-by-pitched-balls, and not a single incident with Bull.

One Baltimore sports caster noted that Homer had been intentionally walked in over thirty percent of his times at bat this season. And that he'd set an all-time record at being hit by pitched balls. Only a handful of those had resulted in bench clearing brawls. The brawls were usually broken up by the time Homer had made his way out to the mound to see what was going on. And the fact was, it really didn't bother him much to get hit by the ball anyway.

Following the Chicago series, the Detroit Lemons came to town for just a two-game series. The Flags won both, and Homer was still batting 1000.

Some unscrupulous media rascals had begun breaking the unwritten rules. They were showing up at Homer's apartment at all hours of the day and night. Homer, who rarely got ruffled, had gotten so frustrated with them at 2:00 a.m. one morning that he had stomped out into the hallway and totally destroyed $28,000 worth of camera and sound equipment, "scaring the devils to hell and gone." It all raised a minor furor in the sports news the following evening, and then quickly died out.

But, in spite of Homer's batting performance, there was enough of a thread for Bull to renew his battle with Flags' management over Homer's future: "Send that idiot to some minor league farm team in Iraq!" Management's concession was to let Bull bench Homer for the opening game with the Philadelphia Lawyers the following night.

The Flags lost the game 6 to 2. With Homer back in the line-up, the Flags won the next two games, but only with considerable controversy. Prior to that second game, the Lawyers had asked for a restraining order to prevent Homer from playing, on the grounds of his egregious and dangerous behavior demonstrated in the camera and sound equipment incident. When that request failed, they filed suit against Homer in district court as "a threat to the visiting team." He was characterized as "an extremely volatile and hostile individual, venomous to the game of baseball, with unremitting criminal tendencies and a grievous menace to those around him."

Although the judge promptly dismissed the suit as frivolous, the whole series had been disrupted from the fans' point of view. The second game had been delayed by nearly three hours, waiting for a decision on the restraining order, and the final game was delayed by an hour over the threats and indecision by the Lawyers regarding their next legal maneuver.

The Baltimore fans were so upset that they vowed to boo the Lawyers, in that third game, even louder than the Philadelphia fans normally did. Although that was not a realistic goal, they did boo loud enough, and long enough, to drown out all P.A. system announcements and the organ's playing of "Take Me Out to the Ball Game" during the seventh inning stretch.

In the end, the Lawyers, predictably, filed formal protests of the two games they'd lost to the Flags – and the season carried on.

The final three games of the home stand were against the Boston Socialists, losers of 34 straight games coming into Ripken Field. This visit extended that to 37. But the Socialists stood proud. A month and a half earlier they had selected a new manager, Jonathan Middlebury.

Two years earlier Jonathan had first met with a group of homeless people near Boston Commons when he was researching "the real source" for a term paper while a senior at Harvard. He was a sociology major, and he intended to reveal to the callous public the plight of the homeless. He quickly became one of them, did not complete his degree, and did not have to scavenge for a job.

On his way back to his townhouse, on several evenings over a two-year period, a PR man for the Boston Socialists had noted that Jonathan was always wrapped in the sports pages of the *Globe*. He thought it novel and casually mentioned it at a staff meeting one morning at the Stadium. The baseball season had gone down the tubes even earlier than usual, and on-schedule the Socialists had fired their manager. Now seeking a replacement, and not wanting to victimize a true future major league manager, the general manager said, "What the hell. Let's bring this homeless guy named Jonathan in for an interview. After all, he may actually be a baseball fan."

Jonathan cooperated. After all, what a whale of a joke to play on those callous people who spend huge sums of money going to baseball games. The PR man was elated. What a publicity stunt to regenerate fan interest.

So in the spirit of Boston Socialist philosophy, the team now had a new manager who'd never attended a major league game, who spoke three languages, and who was a near Harvard graduate -- an unprecedented combination.

It had been a rough start as manager, but Jonathan had engineered some successes. He'd gotten all the handicap access ramps in Socialist Stadium rebuilt and intended to extend that throughout the major leagues. And since his friends from near the Commons didn't qualify for welfare benefits, he arranged to have them included in the various perks the Socialists already offered that segment of the community. And finally, he had begun a campaign to make all major league clubhouse and skybox facilities available to the homeless as winter quarters during the off-season which would be a long one in Boston. And Jonathan became a hero in part of Boston.

But the Baltimore media had pretty much ignored Jonathan during his three games there. After all, they were fully occupied with Homer and Bull. It had been the Flags final home stand of the season. And what a wrap up the *Sun* and the local TV sports casters presented as the Flags waved goodbye to their loyal fans. Well, at least, until the playoffs.

## CHAPTER TWENTY-TWO

# *Wilmington – Mid-September*

The sirens were blaring, and the emergency vehicle horns were honking, and they were all headed up our street. "What the hell's goin' on now?"

I'd often heard them go by down on Chester Street. It was a daily occurrence. But they'd never come up our quiet old street since I'd lived there.

Next thing I hear them stop right in front of our building, doors slamming and sirens phasing down. By the time I'd gotten myself over to the front window, they were rushing through our front door and clattering up the stairs like all hell was falling apart.

It was dark outside. Must have been about 11 o'clock. I'd dozed off and had woken up hearing the racket coming up the street.

I could see an emergency van and two police cars, their red gumballs whirling and radios garbling. Best I could tell about four or five officers and emergency crew headed up the stairs. My first thought was that maybe Dack and the *bitch* had taken an overdose. That seemed like a likely thing. Then deep down – I think I was trying to avoid the thought – what if something happened to one of the kids? My stomach knotted.

I opened my door a crack so I could peak up the stairs without getting my head taken off. Somebody had opened their apartment door after the officers had hammered on it a couple of times. Then they poured into the apartment quickly and closed the door behind them. I could hear some commotion but nothing clear enough to figure out what the hell was going on. Then things went mostly quiet for a while; I thought maybe they'd gotten a handle on things and everything was okay.

I'd just closed my door, so's not to be like a snoop, when down the stairs they came. I got to the front window to see as they came out the front door. First came a cop with a flashlight holding the door open. Then, holy shit!, came the two paramedics toting somebody on a stretcher. It was not an adult. I could tell it was not an adult!

Strange though, there was nobody but the two emergency people and the stretcher. They whipped off quickly, siren howling and lights blinking.

And I was just standing there still churning when down the steps came a big clatter and a bitchy-like male voice protesting whatever was happening. Then out the front door, first a cop, then Dack in handcuffs, then another cop behind. "God, it was good to see them move that rotten bastard out with zero nonsense. But the stretcher? Oh, Christ, which kid was on that stretcher? And how bad? Oh shit! How bad?"

Somehow I'd hoped that fuckin' Dack would try to escape and they would shoot the son-of-a-bitch in the back.

Their apartment door had been left partly open, and I could hear the *bitch* wailing and screaming at the other cop. "He just shook him and shook him and beat him and threw him on the floor!" She was going berserk. That was about all I could make out. She'd kept repeating the same lines over and over again. It sounded as though the cop was trying to settle her down from time to time. But she just kept screaming and wailing.

Then I heard, "If he killed my Bibbie, I'll kill him. I'll kill him!" She was screaming, bitter, very bitter. Then all of a sudden she cooled down and just kept sobbing.

"Ma'am, we'll need to take you and the girl to the hospital. Is this your purse?" The cop's voice was patient and sympathetic. I didn't want to be in his shoes. Then a small burst of sobbing – I could tell that was Arsha. Poor friggin' kid; must have been scared shitless.

And then I thought about Bibbie – little Bibbie.

Then all loaded into the cruiser and headed out. After all that commotion, everything was suddenly quiet – and sickening.

I knew the nearest hospital was only four or five blocks, almost straight up over the hill at the end of our street. At least I hoped that was the hospital they'd gone to.

No way I could go back to bed. My guts were churning. All the rotten things you could think of going on in my head. I can't tell you the horrible sickening feeling I had – Bibbie, Bibbie, you poor little bastard. Oh, Jesus Christ, why hadn't I gotten hold of some agency sooner? Oh, Jesus Christ!"

As much as I despised the *bitch*, I had to pity her now. And Arsha – poor God damned little Arsha. Oh poor damned kid.

I had no choice but to get over to the hospital. Must have taken me an hour to limp those five blocks. I must have destroyed Dack a thousand times on that walk. "God, if I could destroy him just once!"

The woman at the reception desk couldn't give me much information. Yes, they'd admitted a small child in the emergency room about an hour ago. She couldn't give me any information about his condition at this time. And dumb ass me; I couldn't give her his full name. I knew, or at least I thought, his last name was Bogdan. But I didn't really know that for sure. That was just the name I'd seen on their mailbox back at the apartment. And all I knew was "Bibbie." I hadn't ever really thought about his actual name. And I hadn't really paid close attention when Arsha had given it to the cops back at the park zoo a couple months ago.

The handful of sorry-looking people sitting there in the reception area must have thought I was nuts, the way I was behaving. Maybe I shoulda gone straight into the emergency room instead.

# CHAPTER TWENTY-THREE

## *Cleveland – Mid September*

Off to Cleveland and a four-game series with the third place Mistakes. Homer's parents had rented a box to bring a group from New Somerton up to the first game. Around lunchtime Homer went down to the hotel lobby to meet them all, and to sign autographs. He didn't recognize most of them – only a couple from his old high school class. He wished Rodney and Dave could have been with them. But he realized they were off to other things now.

As each player was introduced prior to the game that evening, hundreds of beer cans were flung on to the field. By the time the Cleveland players were ready to take the field, it was virtually coated with aluminum. Then, mysteriously (to Homer), the cans all just seemed to float away.

Jose, sitting next to Homer on the far end of the bench, explained it all.

"See how those cans all disappear into those pits around the edge of the field?"

Homer nodded affirmatively.

"Well, all the way around behind those are huge suction pumps the ball club had installed to just suck the beer cans into the pits – all the way from the center of the field to the edges."

Homer was impressed.

Jose continued, "It's a hallmark here in Cleveland. Since they couldn't change the fans, they changed the stadium. In fact, they're making money on it. From the pits the cans are fed right into a huge set of crushers. Then they're melted down and turned into aluminum ingots. Then they're sold back to the beer can manufacturer at a handsome profit. And the cycle starts all over again, all right here under the stadium. Word is that Joe Brineburner is so envious of the scheme he's trying to think of ways to coax the Capitalist fans into throwing all their cans onto the field in New York."

"Play ball," the ump roared.

In his first at bat, Homer doubled, knocking in two runs. Although those two runs turned out to be the winning margin in the game, Homer was supposed to have taken the pitch. So Bull thoroughly embarrassed him in front of his New Somerton fans by a sarcastic reminder to him as he trotted back across first base en route to the dugout following the third out of the inning.

Homer somewhat redeemed himself – not to Bull, but to his fans – hitting two singles his next couple times at bat. He'd been buzzed half a dozen times by near-bean-ball pitches by Ralph Merser, Cleveland's starting pitcher. So Homer was happy to see a reliever come into the game in the eighth inning.

But with the bases loaded, and only one out, Homer came to the plate, triggering a flood of beer cans onto the field. After a brief vacuuming delay, the game continued.

The first pitch was a curve ball, so vicious that even Homer couldn't duck in time. It caught him right in the groin. His dad was allowed into the visiting team clubhouse to console him as the team physician administered care.

Homer was only out of the lineup for one game, and that was the only game the Flags lost in that Cleveland series. However, he did get an extra day's rest.

The players' union had been doing some sabre-rattling in preparation for upcoming negotiations with the owners over a number of issues. The following evening word came around that the players were all to miss their team bus. In fact, all players, throughout the major leagues, were ordered by the union to be in-absentia that evening. Legal or not, by the time a judge could rule, the games had all been postponed indefinitely.

Homer didn't quite understand it all, so Jose attempted to explain: apparently the more hawkish union firebrands – and Jose was not one of them – were extremely upset with the $300,000 minimum salary. They were demanding it be raised to $500,000. After all, a new Mercedes – at least one suitable for a major league baseball player – was now $75,000. And the whole practice of steroid testing was to be stopped! Immediately! It was interfering with their performance. In fact, there was to be no drug testing of any kind. That would interfere with their recreation. And full, lifetime healthcare benefits were demanded for players, their immediate family members, their parents, grandparents, their grandchildren, all siblings, and all live-ins as well.

The owners, in turn, were demanding conversion of half of all major league teams into a new AAAA minor league category with salary caps of $250,000. They were also demanding that all major league salaries be tied strictly to performance, e.g., if, in any given year a player's performance declined by 25%, so did his salary. Furthermore, all healthcare benefits were to be paid for by the players, and there was to be unlimited, random drug testing.

Homer still didn't understand. He figured the $300,000 he was making this year was more than he'd make in his whole lifetime back in New Somerton. And besides the ball club even paid his plane fare and hotel expenses at the out-of-town games.

The next morning's edition of the *Cleveland Plain Dealer* advocated a fan's union, full refunds on all season tickets, free parking at all major league ball parks -- if they ever did resume baseball – and at least in Cleveland, free beer so as to increase the cans thrown, thus spreading the fixed costs of the vacuum system and can reprocessing equipment under the stadium.

Homer asked Jose if that meant to include free beer for the players.

The Commissioner of Baseball was in a tizzie. This had caught him right in the middle of a decision regarding what to do about the 16 games between the Philadelphia Lawyers and the Washington Bureaucrats which had been postponed for various reasons endemic to those two venues, and which were yet to be played.

And just to complicate things, a disturbing piece of information had been leaked to the press just the day before. According to "informed" sources, the Washington Bureaucrats had recently developed an innovation, to be unveiled next season, whereby umpires would be replaced by a satellite surveillance system which would be capable of calling balls and strikes electronically within one-one-thousandth of an inch accuracy. With a simple sensor system, it could also register all tag outs and throw-outs at the bases as well.

The umpires union immediately threatened to strike – pending further information.

What a mess.

Hoping to generate some excitement, an ESPN camera crew caught Bull and Homer in the hotel lobby. But Bull was under a heavy sedative and couldn't articulate. Homer was not under a heavy sedative and couldn't articulate. So the crew gave up and interviewed Hank and Jose, who were so unemotional and rational about the "work stoppage" that the interview never was aired.

Fortunately, the players were ordered back to play the next evening, and Bull was caught on tape throwing a bat at Homer for swinging at a pitch he was supposed to let go by. The bat missed Homer, hit the home plate umpire, and Bull was ejected. The entire scene was run, and re-run, hundreds of times that evening on every sports news broadcast around the country.

The Flags headed for the airport late that evening with two wins, one loss, and a game suspended while in Cleveland.

On the flight to the West Coast, Bull snorted as he came across some stats in *Baseball Weekly*:

*Homer*
*Batting average: 1000*
*Home runs: 49*
*Runs batted in: 374*
*Intentional walks: 301*
*Hit by pitched balls: 68*
*Caught off base: 98*
*Errors: 15*

Bull observed to Hank, sitting next to him, "15 errors, and he's only played 14 innings of defense all season. What a jerk."

## CHAPTER TWENTY-FOUR

# *Wilmington – Mid September*

"Know anything about all the sirens going on up the street last night?" the woman ahead of me in line was asking the grocer.

"Not any details. Maybe something in the morning paper. But I haven't looked at it yet."

The woman behind me in line cut in, "I heard some guy had beaten up on his girlfriend and her kid. And the cops came and got him."

I paid for my groceries and a copy of the morning paper and headed up the street as quickly as I could make it. I'd gotten up early – couldn't sleep much that night – and had gone down to the grocery to get some stuff for breakfast. Also, I probably was thinking maybe I'd find out something about last night. Maybe the grocer, or some customer, would have heard something. Sure as hell wasn't gonna find out anything back in my building. Couldn't wait to get back and dig through the paper.

Most likely section might be the police reports. Maybe happened too late to make the morning paper.

*ABUSED TODDLER IN CRITICAL CONDITION*

> *A 19-month old boy was in critical condition Thursday night at New Castle Hospital, hours after he was brought to the hospital by paramedics, according to a hospital spokeswoman. William Bogdan, of 973 Riley Street, suffered head injuries and multiple fractures on his body resulting from an apparent act of violence by a male companion of the boy's mother. According to city police officer Charles Rolley, 29-year old Darius Journen was taken into custody at the mother's apartment following a 911 call placed by the boy's older sister. Charges are pending following an investigation.*

I grabbed the phone – misdialed twice, my damned hands were shaking so much. Christ, I was on hold forever. The hospital woman who'd answered my call finally got back with no new information. "He is still in critical condition. " That's all she could tell me.

I just sat. Sat and stared.

A long time later I moved out to my spot on the front stoop. Didn't sit there long though. Didn't want to be there in case the *bitch* appeared.

"Yet, maybe she'd tell me – something."

I walked. And walked. Around blocks I'd never been before. Almost walked down to the hospital. But then opted for the park. I could think there. It was my second home. Maybe I'd go to the hospital later. Maybe later they could tell me something.

I headed for the nearest bench. One I'd sat at many times before. The green paint was getting sort of faded and chipped. Needed a paint job. I sat. The park was quiet. Not very many people around. Lonely. Lonely as hell. The playground and ball fields were all empty. The hot dog vendor was gone for the season. And the carnival was long, long gone.

"Jesus Christ! How is the little bastard? How the hell is he?" I was going nuts.

My hatred of Dack crept back. I hoped they'd sizzle the bastard in an electric chair. And the *bitch* with him. They didn't use electric chairs any more.

Then I wondered about Arsha. What was she doin'? What was she thinkin'? She's gotta be in school right now. But how the hell can she concentrate on school work? Poor fuckin' kid. She's gotta be hurtin'.

An older woman came hobbling down the bike trail. She was moving right along, cane and all. "Good morning." She gave me a great big smile and kept on moving. I guess I said good morning. But I doubt that I smiled. I wished she'd stopped to talk. God, I needed somebody to talk to!

I went back home. Paused just to sit for a moment in my spot; when I had no sooner sat down and a car stops along-side the cars parked in front. And out gets the *bitch*. The car heads off while she slowly makes her way toward the front steps. Not her usual hard-charging pace. Her head was down. She looked so sad I almost had to feel sorry for her. I was torn inside-out what it might mean!

She took hold of the iron porch rail and just stood there at the bottom step. I'd never spoken to the *bitch* before, but she was so pitiful looking I blurted out, "How's Bibbie?"

She looked up at me, glassy-eyed. Her cheeks and the corners of her mouth were quivering. "He may not live." She broke down sobbing and dropped down to one knee, still holding onto the rail.

I did something that 24 hours earlier I'd never believed. I struggled up, went over to her, bent down, and hugged her.

She hung onto the rail with her right arm; with her left arm reached over and hugged me back. She was still sobbing; I was trying to choke back tears.

We were there as long as our knees held up. I finally had to shift; then she stood up, gave me one final hug, and headed in the door and up the stairs.

I sat back down and just sat there – my head in my hands – a long time.

Maybe a half hour later I see, out of the corner of my eye, Arsha coming up the sidewalk with her backpack, head sorta down as though she was concentrating on something.

"Hi, Arsh." She may have said hi back, but she barely glanced at me as she marched straight up the steps, through the door, and up the stairs. She couldn't yet have known what her mother had just told me. But she had to be worried. Wasn't like her to just barge by me like that.

I went on into my apartment, sat down and just thought; about crazy things. Thought about the time when I was a kid and Maggie, my beautiful little sister, drowned in a creek and none of those kids with her would save her; thought about the time there was a riot down the street in Philly. And police vans hauled a bunch of people away, sirens blaring. Thought about that woman at the grocery this morning; "…heard some guy had beaten up on his girlfriend and her kid…" I thought about Bibbie. Chubby little bastard. Big brown eyes looking up at me.

Couple hours passed. Then a light rap on my door. My God, it was Arsha. She was hurting. I knelt down on one knee and reached out to her slowly. She reached out and we hugged. She was sobbing, out of control.

"Come on out front, Arsh." She hesitated for a bit, but I was able to slowly ease her out to the front stoop, still sobbing and shaking; all the time I'm wondering why she came to me. What's up with her mother?

"How's your mother, Arsh?" I was whispering. Between sobs she was able to tell me that her mother had taken some pills and was out asleep.

"Oh shit!" I muttered to myself. This time I got off my butt, like I shoulda done weeks ago, went in and called 911. Amazing. I'd no sooner gotten Arsha settled down to the point where I could explain to her what I'd done when up the street comes the emergency van. They were quick.

"Apartment on the second floor on the right," was all I had time to say.

Arsha was stunned at first; then went into quivering. I grabbed her again and just hugged. I held her fast for a long time. She finally eased down and laid her head between my arm and my ribs.

"We don't think it's serious. We're going to take her in as a precaution. But she'll probably be released this evening."

She was back in less than three hours.

"Everything will be okay, Arsha." She could tell I wasn't very sure about that.

"Bibbie's gonna die!" She burst out bawling and shaking, and God damn it! I just didn't know what to do! I tried to hug her again, but she just pulled away, sobbing out of control.

We stayed out a long time. She finally settled down to a light sob. Once in a while I'd try to say something. But I wasn't doing it very well.

"Shit! What can I say to her?" I was talking to myself again. Lucky, only a couple of older people walked by our sidewalk the whole time. And they didn't pay any attention to us.

It was turning dark. Street lights were coming on, and apartments were lighting up.

"Wanna go inside?"

She gave me a feeble whimper, "No."

I didn't really want to go inside anyway. Didn't want to leave her alone up in their apartment. And didn't think I oughta be up there with her very long. And same reason I didn't feel right about her coming into my apartment. At least the weather was still warm. Thank God for something. "God damn! I wish her mother'd get back."

Maybe it was good I had all that to worry about. Keep my mind off Bibbie. "Holy shit! Oh please God; wherever, please, for Christ's sakes, please! Save the little bastard." I was quietly whimpering, hoping Arsha didn't detect it.

Her mother finally pulled up in a taxi. She looked very tired, very weak. But she seemed calm. A lot more in her senses than before.

## CHAPTER TWENTY-FIVE

# *San Francisco – Late September*

This was Homer's first trip to San Francisco. Unfortunately the flight landed at night during a thick low-lying cloud cover so that he could only see some faint lights somewhere off in the mist.

It was chilly as hell as the players stepped out of the terminal to board their bus. Jose apologized for not warning Homer to wear a jacket there in late summer.

Early that next afternoon Homer went out and bought a pair of thermals to wear under his uniform that evening. Thank goodness. By game time the fog was so thick he wondered if the outfielders would be able to see fly balls.

Eventually the stadium lights burned it away, and the umpire called "play ball."

The Fogs were eleven games out of first place in the Western Division. They were solidly in fourth place with only six games to play. So the crowd was light that evening.

Over the years one local community had cornered most of the season tickets in their three favorite sections (H, I and V) and had developed a practice of using coordinated flash card messages to announce their causes to the fans and to the media. Jose had to interpret to Homer the various metaphors and other indirect meanings of these colorful schemes. Homer thought them a bit strange. But then, what the devil, if that's what turns them on, it didn't much bother him.

Two good things happened, and one bad, in that first game. The first good thing was that the Flags won, extending their Eastern Division lead over the second place New York Capitalists to 19 games.

The second good thing was that Homer went four for four with a double and three singles, knocking in five runs in the 7 to 5 victory.

But the bad thing was so horrible, in Bull's mind, that it nearly cost Homer his career (again), or his life, or both. It was the top of the ninth, and the Flags had the bases loaded with no outs. Homer was the runner on third. The batter popped a high fly ball into short right field. Routine out. Except that the Fogs right fielder and second baseman collided while trying to field the ball. It dropped to the ground, and as the two of them scrambled to retrieve it, the Flags runners on first and second bases headed for second and third, respectively. Problem was that Homer, instead of heading for home, got all confused and headed back to second. Unfortunately, the Flags runner from first had already rounded second. With the three base runners all within twenty feet of each other – Homer still confused and only a couple steps off third – the only triple play of the season was accomplished.

Quick thinking Hank, along with a couple other coaches, managed to get themselves between Bull and Homer just long enough to enable Jose to scoot Homer off the field and into the Fogs' dugout. Jose had spent a couple years in the minors with the Fogs' current manager and was able to quickly plead with him to let Homer use the Fogs' home team clubhouse to shower and change.

Bull, meantime, had gone into such a rage that he was ejected from the game and was escorted into the visiting team clubhouse. A couple other Flags' teammates were able to coax the team physician to get Homer's clothes from his locker. Then they talked the bat boy into getting Homer's stuff over to his fellow bat boy, who in turn got them to the Fogs' clubhouse.

In what Homer's teammates later hailed as "the miracle of the season," Bull had actually come to terms with himself and allowed Homer to play the following afternoon. It was a lovely, sunny afternoon! The fog had yet to set in, and Homer didn't even need the thermals.

And to boot – now hear this Homer fans – the Flags won the game 1 to 0 on a ninth inning homer Homer had blasted over the center field wall. Bull was so pleased that he barely made a disparaging comment about Homer during his post-game interview with the media.

And the *San Francisco Chronicle* bade the Flags farewell with the following sports page headline: "Homer, go home."

As the flight from San Francisco began its approach into the LAX area, a flight attendant made the announcement: "Your flight attendant is now passing out smog masks to be worn while you are in the Los Angeles area. For your own safety please place them over your face the moment you exit the airport terminal. This will be the most hazardous part of your journey. Thank you for flying our airline."

"Better put it on," Jose cautioned Homer as the players passed through the revolving doors to board their bus. "That is, if you hope to play tonight."

These were the final three games of the season for both teams. If the Los Angeles Smogs could win all three, they'd make the playoffs as the Western Division wild card team. So Smog Stadium was jammed that evening.

"Strange-lookin' crowd," Homer posed to Hank during pre-game warm-up. "Looks like thousands of white dots, instead of heads." "Those are just the smog masks, Homer," Hank explained, then quickly slipped his mask back on after talking.

Hank then turned to pick up a stray ball and didn't notice that Homer hadn't slipped his mask back on. And by the time anybody noticed him, Homer was choking and wheezing and writhing on the ground. He'd been without his mask for a full three minutes before the trainer could get the oxygen supply to him.

Bull just shook his head in disgust as Homer was carried off the field on a stretcher. By the time they had revived poor Homer, the game had already begun. As a matter of precaution, the team physicians ordered that Homer remain in the visiting team clubhouse for the remainder of the game. The Flags lost 4 to 0.

The Smogs' fans were ecstatic. If they could now win those final two games, they were in. But they didn't.

Homer managed to keep his mask on, and the Flags won both games, 2 to 1 and 3 to 2, respectively. He got only one hit, a two-run double, to win the second game. But then he got only one official at bat. So he finished the season with the phenomenal unprecedented batting average – 1000!

During those final two games in Los Angeles, he had been intentionally walked eight times and had one ground ball single, scoring the winning run in the second of the two games. To their credit, the Smogs pitching staff had not attempted to hit Homer with a single pitch.

The Smogs then packed their bags for the season, and the Flags headed back to Baltimore for the International Universe League playoffs.

The *Los Angeles Times* described Homer as the "most inept (he had been picked off on this road trip three times), most valuable, dumbest, greatest hitting, designated hitter of all time."

The *Baltimore Sun* offered similar sentiments, and the mayor of New Somerton declared a national holiday.

# CHAPTER TWENTY-SIX

# *Wilmington – Early October*

Had to go down to ask the grocer where the nearest toy store was. Goddamn, it was in the opposite direction from the hospital. Caught the transit bus on the corner. Damned thing was jammed with people still going to work along with three or four school girls in parochial school outfits. At the third stop I had to get off and walk three blocks over to the downtown mall.

Store didn't open 'til 10 a.m., for Chrissake. So I had to cool my heels in a crowded coffee shop for half an hour.

I hadn't shopped for a toy for 100 years. Damn. I couldn't believe the prices. First, I looked at the stuffed animals. Thought something soft and cuddly would be better in a hospital bed. Thought that's what Bibbie would like best. But not a teddy bear. We'd already won one of those. Christ, I couldn't afford half the things.

The woman running the store was very pleasant. Tried to be helpful. We finally settled on a stuffed, fat alligator with a big smile on his face. Bibbie oughta giggle at that. I could feel a lump. I was fighting it back. For Chrissake, the little bastard probably isn't even conscious. I'm on a wishful thinking trip.

I think the woman could tell I was hurting. She seemed sensitive and gently rang up the sale.

I left the store and was about to cross the intersection down the first block when a goddamn old beaten up Pontiac comes around the corner at me. Tires squealing, half out of control with two children in the front seat! Fuck me! The one driving could barely see over the dashboard. She couldn't have been more than 14 or 15. The one in the passenger seat I didn't have time to see. But she was no bigger than the one driving.

I went backwards. Landed against an empty trashcan sitting there next to a utility pole.

"You little bitches!" I screamed at them.

They went tearing on down the street through a yellow light at the next block.

I was embarrassed when a couple women, who'd seen the whole thing, came over to help me up. I was sure they'd heard me.

"You okay, mister?"

"Yeah, yeah, I guess."

They watched me brush myself off. I checked the alligator to make sure he wasn't scuffed.

"Brats that age shouldn't be driving a car."

Back at the apartment I agonized over how to get the alligator to Bibbie. I was sure they couldn't let me in to see Bibbie if I went to the hospital myself. I even called and asked. Nope. Only immediate family.

I didn't want to give it to his mother to take. Didn't know how she'd feel about it. And didn't want to bother her – with all her agonizing worries anyway. And Arsha couldn't be any help. Christ, I hoped Bibbie was getting better.

I went outside – out front. I always wanted to be outside. After years of working in a big shop, noisy with machinery and workers, I couldn't stand to be cooped up in that damn little apartment very long at a time.

It was around noontime. Up the street comes Arsha and her buddy, Bandi.

"School out early today?"

She nodded yes. "The teachers meeting is this afternoon." That's all she said. She and Bandi paused to talk about school girl things.

Arsha never seemed to call me "Mister" any more. Not that I gave a damn. But she seemed more serious now than she had before the school year had started up. Kids change, and they're tough to read.

I'd always thought of Arsha as sorta my buddy, my go-between. Go-between, between Bibbie and me – and between her mother and me; in kind of a distant way, anyway.

Not that she was unfriendly now. But her mind seemed on other things now since Bibbie went to the hospital. And now was when I felt I wanted to talk to her. To find out about Bibbie. Before, she'd probably have told me everything she knew about how he was doing, what her mother had said, and what she was thinking.

Now it was hard to get to even ask her a question. She'd just zip right past me up the stairs, or out the front door and head right off to school, or wherever else she was going.

Except for the paramedic incident, I hadn't seen her mother since I'd hugged her and watched her cry her way up to her apartment. I wondered if she was okay. If I could just get Arsha to pause and talk to me for a moment.

I thought about Bibbie. Somehow I've got to get over there and see him. Or at least talk to a nurse or a doctor who could fill me in.

I didn't think of her as "the *bitch*" any longer. Since I still didn't know her name, I thought of her as "their mother."

I knew she had to be coming and going. We simply hadn't crossed paths. She had to be going to the hospital. This was the fourth day now. I wondered if she was going to work these days. Poor damned woman.

I hadn't seen anything about Dack in the papers. Of course I didn't read the paper regularly, or very carefully. Besides, there were probably ten more nasty child abuse cases since Bibbie.

I'm pondering all this – must have been about noontime – I looked down the street, just gazing around you know, and here comes Arsha. She was walking very slowly. Just kind of meandering. Looking sort of sad and fidgety. I don't think she saw me sitting there 'til she got up close to our building. Her mind was somewhere else. Took her a long time to work her way up the sidewalk.

"Arsha?"

She looked pretty down, so I tried to be gentle.

"Arsha? You okay?"

She paused, kept looking down at the sidewalk, and slowly shook her head no.

"What's wrong?" I guess I was thinking that it was all over Bibbie, but I wondered what the hell she was doing home from school in the middle of the day.

She put her backpack down and sat down on the step, the other side of the stoop below me. From an angle, I could see tears coming up.

I scooted down next to her, hoping like hell she wouldn't just get up and leave.

"Arsha? Talk to me. What's up?" Again, I tried to be as gentle as possible.

"Did school let out early today?" I knew it hadn't, because she was the only kid in sight.

After a long pause and a couple of sobs, she finally got it out. "The teacher sent me home." Then some more sobs.

"Why'd she do that?"

"She said if I wasn't going to do my school work I'd just have to go home and think about it." She broke down sobbing quite a while.

"Didn't she call your mother?" I asked her once she settled down a little.

"She sent a note." She choked that out.

"Well, didn't she make sure somebody was coming to meet you? So that you wouldn't be walking home alone?"

"I told her I'd called my mother, and she was coming." The sobs kept coming.

I waited a little bit, then asked her, "But did you call her?"

"No, I just walked home." She broke down sobbing again.

I waited longer this time. Tried to figure out how to get her mind off her school stuff. I took a risk: "Do you know how Bibbie's doin'?" Then I chewed on my lip and waited.

Thank God she finally whimpered out, "Mother's taking me to the hospital today to see him." Then we sat there quiet a long time.

"Arsha, would you ask your mother if I could go along? I'll pay for the taxi."

Arsha came back down a half hour later to tell me that would be okay.

Nobody said anything on the way to the hospital. "Damn it." I realized I'd forgotten the alligator. I paid the driver and we headed into the reception area.

At first they weren't going to let Arsha up to the critical care because of her age. Then there was a phone call. And then all three of us were allowed to go up. They didn't even ask me who I was. Must have thought I was an uncle or something.

Through some corridors, stopped at a nurses' station; then a nurse led us down another corridor and into the room where Bibbie was.

I thought I was gonna choke open. Poor little bastard looked awful. All bandaged up, unconscious, with tubes running into him. God, what a pathetic sight.

Nobody said anything. We just stood there, kind of stunned. His mother was the only one who'd seen him before. We all had tears running down our cheeks.

Then the doctor came in. He took Bibbie's mother aside to say something to her in private. I looked at the nurse. "It doesn't look good," she half whispered. I don't think Arsha heard her. The poor kid was over concentrating on Bibbie and was sobbing lightly.

Next thing I hear from around the corner is Bibbie's mother breaking out wailing and sobbing and pleading with the doctor, and with God, to "do something, do anything, to save my baby!"

It was a sad trek from the taxi up the steps and into our building. I said goodnight, and they went slowly up the stairs and into their apartment.

I didn't know what the doctor had said to his mother, but it must have been just a more detailed version of what the nurse had whispered to me. I sat down in the gloom of my crappy little apartment and choked back tears, fighting a big lump in my throat.

I went for a walk. I'd never walked the area before after dark. Down past the corner grocery. Must have been a dozen people in there. I could see the grocer through the plate glass windows. Standing there behind his register, chatting with customers; reaching for a pack of cigarettes for one, a box of something for another, and quickly making change as he went.

What a hell of a long day he goes. Here it's 8:30 at night, and the guy is in there opening at 7:00 a.m. every day. I'd seen him several times when I'd go down to get the morning paper and a cup of coffee.

At the far left of the store I could see a guy with three brats. He was trying to do his shopping while keeping his eye on them. One had just pulled a pack of cookies open and spilled some on the floor. His dad hadn't seen that yet. The kid's younger brother was squalling about something. Meantime I could see their sister -- must have been about four years old – off wandering away toward the other end of the store with the dad looking all over for her. How the hell could the guy go grocery shopping with those brats? His wife must have sent him. I'd have refused.

I had to move on. It was pissing me off.

I decided to turn and go back the other direction where I hadn't ever walked before. I'd passed by on the bus a couple of times, but hadn't noticed the little mini-mall on the corner a block down.

I peered in the laundromat at the near end. A woman, maybe in her thirties, was sitting there on one of those puke green plastic chairs. She was just looking straight ahead. Stone-faced, no expression at all. No movement. I wondered what she was thinking.

A younger woman was sitting a few chairs away. Same thing; just looking straight ahead. No expression, dull eyes. Another woman was up at a machine, sorting laundry, yet with the dullest, blankest expression of all. An older man sat in the rear corner with his face down in his palms, elbows on knees. Looked almost like he was crying.

What a shit awful day these people must all be having.

I paused a couple of stores down to look in the windows of one of those game arcades. A dozen or so kids in there. Brats of all ages, mostly boys; trying to beat the machines. Some looked mean, some looked conniving, and some looked blank. All in there, trying to beat the machines. And when they finished that, half of them would probably go out of the arcade and look for trouble.

I left.

# CHAPTER TWENTY-SEVEN

# *Baltimore – Early October*

The flight from LAX back to Baltimore landed on time at BWI. But it sat on the runway for three hours. Reason was, greeting fans had backed up traffic so far that travelers hoping to board departing flights could not get to the airport. So they all got on their cell phones to let the airline know of their dilemma. The airlines, hungry to fill every seat, delayed the departures, tying up all the gates, preventing arriving flights from getting to their gates to disembark.

All arteries leading into BWI were jammed. The Baltimore-Washington Expressway was a parking lot from the Inner Harbor to the Washington Beltway. And the Washington Beltway was always a parking lot. So was the Baltimore Beltway, as was I-95 from the Washington Beltway to the Delaware State line.

To solve the problem -- traffic control had a departing aircraft located at the end slot of a concourse backed off into a holding area. They then allowed the Flags' flight to jump the line of 23 arriving flights, pull into that open slot, and disembark.

To Bull's dismay, Angelo Peters, never at a loss for a publicity extravaganza, had the team actually exit up through the concourse jammed with thousands of fans. Thus, it took another hour just to get all the players onto a waiting bus. The decibel level was deafening. And in spite of police protection, Homer's shirt was, piece-by-piece, slowly shredded from his back by souvenir- seeking fans. Placards reading *Homer is a Homer to Baltimore* and *Bull Baltimore Replaces Bull Durham*, were waving in the crowd.

And as soon as the team bus had departed, those same fans headed straight to Ripken Field to wait in line for two days for opening playoff game tickets.

After two days of round-the-clock police protection, Homer was relieved to get to the safety of the ballpark. Well, sort of safe. The pitching staff of the Seattle Decafs was loaded for bear. Or at least for Homer.

The starting left-hander was the ugliest human being Homer had ever seen. Big and hairy and snarling. At Homer's first at bat, his first pitch was right on target – Homer's left rib cage.

As Homer dropped to his knees in pain, the biggest bench-clearing brawl of the season ensued. Once both teams had been scooted back into their respective dugouts, and hundreds of fans back into their seats, a stretcher was brought out to remove big, ugly, hairy snarler to the visiting team clubhouse for repairs. And Homer was on first.

The next time Homer came to the plate, the score was tied 2 to 2. In the bottom of the third, with runners on first and third, the crowd was chanting, "Homer, Homer, Homer….."

The first pitch was high and outside. Homer figured he could have hit it had he really wanted to, but with his ribs still aching a little, he decided to take "ball one."

The next pitch was neither high nor outside; it was right at his vitals. He managed to turn just enough that it nailed him in the left hip. Down he went.

The benches cleared again. But this time three rabid, big, ugly, hairy, snarling – and very fast – Flags' fans had anticipated the incident. And they were on the Decafs' pitcher long before his catcher could even get his mask off.

The angry and charging players from both dugouts stopped in their tracks, only midway to the mound – stunned.

The second Decafs' pitcher of this still young game was removed to their clubhouse on a stretcher. And Homer was on first.

Now Homer was not gun-shy when he came to bat for the third time. Bottom of the sixth, two on and two out. He figured their right hander didn't want to be the third Seattle pitcher to exit on a stretcher.

For whatever unexplainable reason, Seattle chose not to go with an intentional walk. First pitch, low and outside, ball one. Next pitch, low and outside. In that flash of an instant, the batter has to make a decision. Homer had concluded they were trying to bait him. It worked! Homer swung.

The bat splintered into a dozen pieces as the ball went screwballing into right field, taking a series of crazy bounces off into the grass along the fence. The right fielder bobbled it twice, both he and the ball bouncing off the wall, as two runs scored and Homer made it all the way to first base.

In his next two times at bat, Homer was intentionally walked.

By the final tally, Homer had scored twice, once from first base on a home run by Bo Monica and once from third base on a bases loaded walk. He had collected two RBIs, was forced out twice at second base, and was stranded once at first.

The Flags won that game 6 to 5.

They won the following evening 17 to 3.

And as they departed for Seattle for the deciding game(s) – and it only took one more – as many fans saw them off at BWI as had greeted them four days earlier. The highways were a mess, flights were delayed, and the Seattle Decafs were rattled.

Homer didn't get one hit in the game at Seattle. That was because he was intentionally walked all four times he was at bat.

Baltimore took all three games, and the first round of the playoffs.

And in the crowning glory of Baltimore baseball history, the Flags swept the New York Capitalists (who had only sneaked into the playoffs as the wild card anyway) in the League Championship Series, four straight games.

The *Baltimore Sun* had prepared to publish a special edition to celebrate. But all its employees from the managing editor on down skipped work for the entire 48-hour extravaganza which jammed the entire area from the Inner Harbor to Ripken Field.

Bull had been tucked away under light sedatives, in an undisclosed location. The players had been counseled as to how to remain in hiding.

But Homer. Well, Homer was Homer, as you might say.

From his 32$^{nd}$ floor living room window, Homer could see all the activity below.

And he wanted to be a part of it.

At the same time as Homer was headed down the elevator, a group of his fans had arrived out front of his building. They had with them an elaborate sedan chair they had constructed with a replica model of Homer one of them had built to honor him.

Never had they expected the thrill of the real Homer appearing. Off went the model into the gutter and up onto the sedan chair went Homer with the assistance of four of his most ardent fans. And off they went marching down the street through the crowds of adoring spectators, right to the heart of the celebration.

Homer tried to explain that the Flags hadn't won the World Series yet, only the League Playoffs – even he understood that distinction – but he was totally ignored; the roars of the thousands prevailed: "Homer! Homer! Homer! ...."

Meantime, Bull's wife was watching the celebration on TV and made the mistake of beckoning Bull to "Come see this!" After the TV set and several other pieces of furniture had been destroyed, she managed to get a Bull-size dose of sedative into him and proceeded upstairs to see the action on a different set.

Fortunately, the Baltimore police chief quickly grasped the implications of Homer's sedan chair appearance and managed to get that phase of the celebration steered back over toward Homer's apartment building.

As Homer was sported past the doorman into his building on the shoulders of two of Baltimore's finest (and biggest), he waved his appreciation to the cheering throngs and settled off to a good night's sleep. And with Homer's parting the attention of the crowd was suddenly drawn to the mysterious arrival of an old-time beer wagon offering free cups of beer to loyal Flags fans from its series of taps pouring from the over-size barrel shaped vat. This, of course, was a gross violation of city ordinances and was abruptly cut-off as soon as the vat had run dry.

What was the city to do for an encore if the Flags were to win the Series? In retrospect the *Sun* wished it had not posed that question.

Two nights later the team had been snuck out of Baltimore on a 2:00 a.m. flight taking them southwest for their opening World Series encounter with the Houston Hydrocarbons. The Hydrocarbons had had to struggle all seven games against the Cincinnati Wursts to take their League title, so the Flags had enjoyed a couple days' rest.

The first two games were to be in Houston before returning to Baltimore for the next three, if the Flags needed that many to accomplish a sweep.

Homer was ready. His teammates were ready. And Bull was ready.

Following morning, *Houston Chronicle* front page headlines: "Players Union Strike Threatens World Series!"

The Flags had been so focused on winning their League playoffs that even Pokey Perry, their union player representative, had lost track of the failing negotiations between the players and the owners.

Angelo Peters was in angst. Bull was livid. And Homer was confused. Call the strike next year, not this year.

But the strike was called.

It had been a great rookie season for Homer. And after all, so he didn't get to play in a World Series, he was now the all time batting champion in the major leagues.

Bull was named "Manager of the Year." And Angelo Peters had given each player a free mini-van (last year's model) as a consolation for the money they would have received had the Series been played.

If the weather is nice in early October, and it usually is, New Somerton is a pleasant place just to walk your dog out through the early autumn scenery. The *Sun* had sent a reporter out to interview Homer; to get his thoughts on the aborted World Series; to record the unbearable agony he'd suffered at such a catastrophic end to his rookie season.

But it really hadn't bothered Homer very much. Even to learn that, the reporter had had to tag along with Homer and Rover out through the woods for a couple of days. He'd tried to plant statements, ask leading questions, and even attempted to embarrass Homer into some emotional reaction. Homer would just sit down on some large tree branch that had fallen, give a sly grin, scratch Rover's tummy, and reminisce some experiences he and Jose had had fighting off admiring girls back in Baltimore.

No anger. No frustration. Nothing sensational for the poor reporter to latch onto.

Thus, while the first four pages were devoted to excoriating the players' strike, only a minor headline of a brief article back on page 5 of the sports page that following weekend: "And Homer is still batting 1000."

# CHAPTER TWENTY-EIGHT

# *Wilmington – Late October*

I didn't see Arsha or her mother at all next morning 'til there was a rap on my door about 10 o'clock. It was Arsha. "Could you take me to the hospital?" She was trembling a little.

"What the hell's going on?" I thought to myself. I guess I just looked at her for a while.

I could see a tear start. I was befuddled, and I think for an instant I feared the worst. "Yeh, yeh; let me grab my wallet," I mumbled.

"What's up, Arsh? What's happening?," as I half stumbled out the door.

"My mother's rushed off to the hospital and forgot to take me with her," she paused. "She was going to take me with her." Poor kid sounded awful meek.

I think I was trembling. "Let's walk down to the corner. Lots of cabs go by there. Be quicker than calling one and having to wait."

"Is everything okay?" I asked.

"I don't know. But she said I could go with her," Arsha whispered, choking lightly.

Neither of us said anything else the whole way over. I was dying. How could her mother just rush out and forget her like that?

I explained to the hospital receptionist why we were there. Then we sat and waited. Christ, we must have waited a half an hour. Finally, a woman came out of the elevator and talked to the receptionist for a moment. She nodded toward us, and the woman came over – she must have been a nurse, I guess.

"Mr. Minley?"

"Yes, ma'am."

"I need to talk with you for a moment. Could you wait here for just a little bit, and we'll be right back?" She spoke very gently to Arsha.

"Mr. Minley, the child passed away at 9:17 this morning." She was very tender. I don't now remember what else she said. Something about his mother, and how...... and his sister, and ...........

* * * *

Dammit Bibbie! Dammit, dammit! Why, why, why, you...? God dammit, Bibbie!

Breinigsville, PA USA
04 February 2010
231938BV00001B/2/P